D0919717

Pony Soldiers

SLAUGHTER AT BUFFALO CREEK

Chet Cunningham

White Eagle was on the warpath. No one was safe – not even Captain Colt Harding's wife and son. They were killed and mutilated; his four-year-old daughter was captured by the fierce Comanche warrior. Burning with hatred, and thirsting for revenge, Harding mounted up his men and began a long bloody trek that would continue until he had seen White Eagle's corpse rotting in the desert sun – until he had rescued his daughter from brutal Indian slavery.

PONY SOLDIERS

SLAUGHTER AT BUFFALO CREEK

Chet Cunningham

Curley Publishing, Inc.
South Yarmouth, Ma.

Library of Congress Cataloging-in-Publication Data

Cunningham, Chet.
Pony soldiers: slaughter at Buffalo Creek / Chet Cunningham.
p. cm.
1. Comanche Indians—Fiction. 2. Large type books. I. Title.
[PS3553.U468P64 1990]
813'.54—dc20
ISBN 0-7927-0280-8 (lg. print) 89-28789
ISBN 0-7927-0281-6 (pbk. : lg. print) CIP

Published in Large Print by arrangement with Dorchester Publishing, Inc. in the United States, Canada the U.K. and British Commonwealth.

Distributed in Great Britain, Ireland and the Commonwealth by CHIVERS LIBRARY SERVICES LIMITED, Bath BA1 3HB, England.

Printed in Great Britain

SLAUGHTER AT BUFFALO CREEK

Chapter 1

Corporal Alf Lewton stared at the rolling plains around him and shook his head.

"Know what I know, Sarge, and *I sure as hell felt them savages*. They watching us, I still say so, and it's a raiding party sure as hell. We should find a spot we can defend and ride out a patrol."

Sergeant Bill Bowers sent a long stream of tobacco juice squirting into the Texas sage. He had been with the Troop since it was formed back in fifty-five. There wasn't much in the way of soldiering and fighting he hadn't seen, including the Comanche.

"Alf, you don't shoot a Comanche until you see the little bastard. Half the time you never see them. You damn well won't see them until they want you to. So we keep moving. If we pull up here, we'll be a day late getting into Fort Comfort and the old man will raise all bloody hell."

Corporal Lewton slouched lower in his saddle where he sat the army black. He looked at his anchors, the three big Pittsburgh supply wagons, each with five thousand pounds of supplies. Then there was the real problem, the fourth rig, a covered wagon that held the most precious cargo, the wife and two small children of Captain Colt Harding, the fort's commanding officer.

Fort Comfort wasn't exactly a hardship post, but damn few women had elected to come into the wilds of Western Texas. It was the last fort before the country turned into the raw and unmapped Comanche hunting grounds.

Alf wanted to light his pipe but he didn't. It was hot enough already and not yet ten o'clock in the morning. He shaded his hand over his gray campaign hat with the low crown and wide brim. It did a lot to keep the sun out of his eyes. He stared at the small sandstone ridge to their right.

True he had not seen any Comanches. He had not even seen smoke there. No Indian smoke signals. He'd heard about them but never actually spotted any. Damn, he wished they were out of this long narrow valley. That is if you can have a valley without any hills. The country was so damn flat it gave him the shakes. He was a Tennessee mountain man himself, and damn proud of it.

Alf loved riding with the Cavalry, the famous Second Cavalry, the sharpest, most highly decorated outfit in the whole damn U.S. Army! Corporal Lewton looked at the ridge of sandstone again, then went back to the head of the small supply train where he rode the point of a fifteen man Cavalry escort.

Eight members of the escort detail were ahead of the rigs, the rest along the sides and a rear guard.

Alf would be damn glad to get in two more good days of travel and arrive at the gates of Fort Comfort. It was called a Fort but was not the headquarters of a regiment. It was more of an outpost over a hundred and twenty miles west of Austin.

Inside the rocking, jolting covered wagon, Milly Harding was trying to read a story to her two children. Little Sadie was just past her fourth birthday. Captain Colt Harding, her father, tried not to show it, but plainly favored the shy little beauty. She had long blonde hair and sparkling blue eyes, a mischievous grin and a laugh that won everyone's heart in a minute. She looked up at her mother now.

"Why is it so hot? Why are we bouncing so much? Mommie, why did we have to leave St. Louis?" The questions were softly spoken, laced with a smile of confusion.

Milly had answered the same questions a dozen times on the long trip, most of it done on the more comfortable stage coaches. Now she smiled and pushed back her own long blonde hair that Colt wouldn't let her cut. She had washed her hair last night and was too tired to put it up properly. Now it swung around her shoulders and half way down her back.

She watched Sadie with eyes that matched the child's intense blue ones and smiled.

"We're going because Daddy wanted us to! Isn't that wonderful! A lot of places Daddy has to work aren't nice enough for sweet little girls and jumping jack boys to stay. But Fort Comfort is the best one so far. And we'll be there in just two more days!"

"I liked it back home," Sadie said shyly. Then she shrugged. "I know I'll like it at our new house too. Won't I, Mommie?"

"Yes you will, Sadie. Fort Comfort is your new home. You'll love living there."

Yale, seven now and the big brother and man-of-the-family when Daddy was away, launched his own worry.

"I sure won't have many kids to play with. Didn't you say there were only two other officers' families there?"

"Yes, Yale, but we don't know how many children they have. Remember the Johnsons? They have twelve little ones."

Yale tried to spin a top on a board but the top, made from a wooden spool for thread, kept falling off the side.

"I hope they both have twelve kids. If not I'm gonna play with the enlisted kids. Maybe I can play with some Indians!"

"Yale Harding, you will not. Indians are savages. That is no way to talk. I'm sure there will be plenty of playmates. Anyway, you'll be able to take riding lessons. Your father promised."

Yale twisted his face, nodded and concentrated on the top.

Milly watched him a moment, he was so like his father, single minded, determined . . . yes, stubborn, a good strong Harding stubborn streak that was evident in both her children. She looked back at Sadie, her beautiful little daughter, and her last child, the doctor had told her.

Sadie was such a love. She seldom complained, almost never got into mischief or trouble, and was as pretty as a picture in her little calico dress and blue ribbons in her long blonde hair. Milly was so thankful to have a sweet little girl. She was the luckiest woman alive! She hugged both her children.

"Now, where were we in the story? Yes, the old fox was in the garden waiting to see if the chicken coop would be closed tightly that night by Farmer Brown."

Milly heard a whoop outside. Yale scrambled over the mattress laid in the bottom of the wagon to the tailgate and looked out the round opening made by the canvas top.

"Something is happening!" Yale called.

Milly walked on her knees to the back of the wagon and pushed her head outside.

The wagon had stopped. The Cavalrymen were shouting. She saw the soldier escort milling around Sergeant Bowers. He looked to the west, and when Milly stared that way she gasped and pushed her hand to her mouth.

Coming down the small rise a quarter of a mile away were at least twenty screaming, shouting Indian braves. She had never seen an Indian before, but these must be Indians, and they were coming to attack the wagons!

Bowers barked orders, dismounting the Pony Soldiers, spotting them behind the wagons. Their breech loading, single shot rifles loaded and ready to fire.

The Comanches came at the supply train in their traditional attack method, a sweeping V with the best war chief riding on the point of the V, his war shield held up as powerful medicine to ward off the roundeyes' bullets.

The Cavalry mounts were tied to wagon wheels and the blue shirted troopers lay behind the wheels to fire at the coming charge. Some of the recruits snapped shots at the raiders.

"Hold your fire!" Bowers bellowed. "Wait until the bastards get within good range, damnit!"

Bowers wished his men had been issued the Spencer repeating rifle like some of the troops had. The seven shot, lever operated weapons, could hold off an attack. His men had a variety of single shot breech loaders and even some muzzle loaders left over from the Civil War.

"God damn, forgot about the civilians!" Bowers yelped and charged to the covered wagon with the passengers and barked in the back opening.

"Mrs. Harding. You lay down low as you can get and keep your kids down. Pile anything you have round you that will stop bullets. Stay in the wagon and keep that pistol handy. Then you better start praying!"

He saw the startled look on the woman's face as she poked her head out of the opening. Then he was gone, diving under her wagon, unlimbering his Gallager breech loading carbine. It was a .52 caliber but the range was no more than 500 yards. He had to wait to fire to be sure the hostiles were in range of all the carbines his men had.

Bowers watched the painted heathens charging forward. When they were within four hundred yards he gave the order to fire, and a dozen rifles barked. Two Indian horses went down. He saw one brave wounded, but the attackers drove forward. On some unseen signal they parted and half went each way as they began circling the line of four wagons.

Only three or four of the Indians had rifles, Bowers decided. But that only made them more deadly – they had to get in close to use their arrows and lances. The sergeant had seen Comanches attacking before, and he was always amazed by their horsemanship. They rode so they were almost entirely hidden on the far side of their charging ponies. They shot their arrows and rifles from under the belly of the horses! There was nothing to shoot at except the Indian pony, which Bowers did now and brought one down.

The Comanche riding the mount rolled away, his bow and arrows held in his right hand. A moment later he vanished behind a small bush, but Bowers knew the savage would be crawling forward still on the attack.

The Indians' circle came closer and closer, sometimes at less then fifty yards, but still there was little to shoot at except the ponies. Some of the Cavalrymen didn't want to kill the mounts. Horses were precious to them.

When the Comanches made their first circle, the troopers had moved between the wagon wheels, where they had some protection from both sides.

The first time the Comanches circled also brought the death of six army horses. The Indians knew if the Pony Soldiers were on foot they would be easier to run down and kill.

Bowers bellowed over the firing for the men to shoot the horses out from under the Comanches, but still few did. The horse was almost sacred to the newer recruits, and Bowers had six of them on this escort duty.

Bowers felt the thud of the arrow but no pain in his back as a lucky shot arrow slanted between the wooden wagon wheel spokes behind him and plunged into his flesh. Funny that it didn't hurt, must be a slanting blow he decided. Bowers tried to lift his carbine to aim it, but his hand wouldn't move.

"God damn!" Bowers screeched. He couldn't move either arm. He tried to sit up only to find that he couldn't move his legs. Christ! The arrow must have hit his spinal column! He was paralyzed! Only his eyes would move and he could talk.

"Lewton, get over here!" Bowers bellowed. A lull in the firing let his voice reach out to the corporal who dashed from the second wagon and slid in beside his superior.

"Yeah Sarge?"

"I'm hit, can't move!"

Alf Lewton looked at the arrow in Bower's back and swore.

"I can't touch it, Sarge. It's deep in your spine. You stay right there. We'll get rid of these damn Comanches and we'll put you in the wagon."

Just as Corporal Lewton said the words, a .52 caliber bullet from Walking White Eagle's rifle slammed through the Pony Soldier's left eye, killing him instantly, dumping him half over Bowers.

The firing diminished. Troopers called to each other as they used up the sixty rounds they carried for their rifles and carbines. Pistols began to fire when the rifles ran dry.

Inside the last wagon, Milly Harding lay on top of her two children, tears of fright and worry streaming down her face as she listened to the fight rage outside. She heard the rifles firing less and less. She could not look outside. Already three arrows had slapped through the canvas top.

The troopers would defeat them, she was sure. Indians were well known to strike and pull back, to strike again and if the defense was too strong, they would pick up their dead and wounded and move to an easier target. It was talked about all the time by the officers' wives who had men fighting the Indians.

These Comanches were savages and cowards and fought only when they had surprise and three times as many Indians as Cavalrymen.

Another arrow sliced through the canvas and tore into her left arm, missed the bone and came out the far side.

Little Sadie began to cry.

Yale squirmed from under his mother and looked at the blood on his mother's arm. The point had gone all the way through with the bloody metal tip sticking in the mattress. Milly shuddered, a soft weeping from the sudden pain flooded from her.

Yale's eyes went wide for a moment, then he swallowed hard. He took both hands and without a word broke off the feather end of the long shaft. Milly choked down a scream when the shaft moved in her flesh.

Yale lifted her arm, grasping the arrow just above the point and suddenly jerked the arrow shaft through the bloody wound and free. Milly screeched in pain, then covered her mouth, tears welling as she tried to control the agony.

"It will be fine now, Mother," Yale said. "I heard Father talking about how to do this," he said solemnly. Then he tied his kerchief around the wound to stop the bleeding.

Milly looked at him with wonder. "Thank you, darling." She shivered, beat down the pain and then pulled her precious children to her. They lay down, pushing as low as they could get and piled bags and boxes on top of them.

Outside under one of the big Pittsburgh freight wagons, Private Templeton fired his Gallager and then pushed a new Poultney foil cartridge in and aimed again. Just before he fired, he saw an Indian break from the pack and ride straight for him. Templeton tried to change his aim, but it was too late.

The fourteen-foot lance the warrior threw from twenty feet away, shot from his hand, flew between the wagon wheel spokes and drove through Private Templeton's throat. He jolted backward, his last shot going wild as he died.

Under the next freight wagon Private Zedicher screamed at his buddy six feet away. "Zeek, you got any more .52 caliber rounds!"

Zeek couldn't reply. He lay as if he were firing his pistol, but a Comanche arrow still quivered where it had driven six inches into Zeek's forehead.

Zedicher saw Zeek's head clearly then, bellowed in rage and jumped up from under the wagon and ran for his horse. It was one of two U.S. Cavalry blacks still standing.

A riderless Indian pony raced toward him. Zedicher waved his pistol at it, but the animal came on. Zedicher couldn't understand it. Then at the last second he saw the buckskin fringed legging showing where an Indian's foot was wedged under the wide rawhide surcingle around the horse.

In a second and a half the Comanche brave lifted up, leaned over his charging pony's back and his knife sliced Private Zedicher's throat from one side to the other. Zedicher died before he fell to the prairie grass.

The brave wheeled, rode upright looking for more yellow legs. He saw only two still firing, and both were about to be cut to pieces by his brothers. The brave rode back, slid off the back of the pony to the body of the yellow-leg-who-ran-away.

Fox Paw made two quick cuts around the Pony Soldier's head, then popped off the short hair. He tucked the scalp under his horsehair belt, then vaulted on his mount and rode toward the last wagon with the tall cover.

There would be much loot to claim and he wanted to be the first in the richest looking wagon.

He leaped from his horse to the wagon's wooden side and sliced the thin canvas with his knife, tearing it back.

Milly Harding lifted the revolver when she saw the savage leap on the wagon. She aimed the heavy six-gun and when the Comanche's face peered through the rent in the wagon cover, she fired. The bullet went wide. She closed her eyes and fired again and the brave slammed backward off the wagon.

Walking White Eagle spun his pony around when he saw Fox Paw fly off the covered wagon. Blood gushed from his shoulder. The last of the Pony Soldiers was down. White Eagle touched his knees to his borrowed war pony and raced up to the rear opening of the last prairie schooner.

In a graceful leap, the Indian went through the covered wagon's small rear opening and came up with his knife in his hand and pressed it against the throat of a white woman. She had no warning, no time to lift the heavy six-gun. White Eagle knocked the pistol from her hand as his knife pushed her back on the mattress.

The two children scuttered to the far end of the wagon and wailed in terror. White Eagle picked up the pistol, it was one of the fires-many-times weapons. He put it in the rawhide band that circled his waist, then caught the woman's long blonde hair and pulled her toward the rear canvas opening.

He threw the woman outside for the braves and turned back toward the children. The boy screamed at him in fury and charged at White Eagle with a pocket knife. White Eagle let the boy come, then suddenly held out his own knife with a six-inch blade. Yale Harding could not stop. He screamed as he staggered and fell on the knife. It penetrated his chest and his heart, killing him instantly.

White Eagle pushed the small boy away without looking at him again and wiped his blade on the boy's clothes. The boy child was too old to train properly. He walked over the carefully packed household goods to the small girl who screamed in gasping, wide-eyed terror.

He picked her up and held her under one arm as he sorted through the goods in the wagon. He found ribbons, a dozen different kinds that he took for his wives, then a long streamer of cloth as wide as his arm. He wrapped the cloth around his torso, took the pistol and a rifle he had found and leaped to the ground.

The white girl was still under his arm, struggling and kicking. He slapped her gently, and she stopped screaming.

Fox Paw had bound up his shoulder wound and had claimed the blonde roundeye woman. He had stripped her clothes off until she was naked, then staked her hands to the ground and spread eagled her legs, tying them to stakes driven in the ground.

With great ceremony he removed his breechclout and dropped between the woman's white thighs. She screeched at him, calling him every vile name she could remember. He slapped her, then twisted her breasts until she screamed in agony.

He drove into her quickly, grunting and panting as three braves stood watching.

The other braves looted the freight wagons. They turned out to be army supply rigs loaded with food and material for the fort. There were many hundred pound sacks of beans, flour, sugar, potatoes, new uniforms, small axes and thousands of items for the Fort Sutter's store.

White Eagle quickly looked at the goods in the wagon. They were three days ride from the safety of the upper Brazos River. They had come far into Texas this time raiding. With any good medicine they could drive one of the wagons closer to their camp. At once he rejected the plan. No brave would drive a wagon, that was woman's work.

A new plan came quickly, it would work. He looked at the stacks of uniforms the braves were throwing around. He caught one pair of blue pants. By cutting the legs off he could use them for winter leggings. He found two more pair and tied them to his mount.

The squalling child under his arm bit his shoulder. He whacked her with the back of his hand. He had forgotten about her. Quickly he tied her hands and feet together with rawhide, then stretched her across his back like a blanket roll and tied a wide rawhide thong from her hands to her feet across his chest. She would be secure there and leave both his hands free for looting.

When he got back to the big covered wagon, the braves had thrown out everything, even the mattress. Two more braves had taken their turn with the white captive, laughing and joking about her blonde muff of crotch hair.

Fox Paw made certain that everyone understood she was his captive and he had claimed her. White Eagle shrugged. It was the way of the People. She would be a difficult slave, but with good training she might do. Even the roundeyes had slaves. He never thought twice about taking slaves or captives or killing hostages. It was simply the way of the People.

White Eagle kicked through the goods from the wagon. He had no need for dresses or clothes. His women would enjoy the ribbons and the cloth he found. He uncovered a copper kettle. It would be good for boiling stew, he tied it to the horse's surcingle and kept looking.

From a small chest he found a round mirror with silver on the handle and a picture on the back. He put it in the kettle and tied it securely.

Also in the chest White Eagle discovered a leather bag filled with cartridges for the revolver. There were over a hundred of them. He smiled as he took them. The fires-many-times small weapon would help make the Comanche as well armed as the Pony Soldiers. Every Pony Soldier had one.

He ran from one of the blue shirted soldiers to the next, picking up the revolvers. Soon he had found them all! It was the best loot he could imagine! He stripped the pistol rounds from the men's pouches and pockets until he had more than he could carry. He filled the copper pot with them, and motioned to Thunder Dog to collect the long guns.

All would be tied securely on a mule to be taken back to the lodges. Soon there was a contest among the braves to find the rifles and carbines, and to locate as much ammunition as they could. They checked each wagon, but there was no more ammunition.

White Eagle called a small council and the

senior warriors stood to one side with their war ponies.

In quick order they decided what must be done. The Pony Soldiers' beans, flour and potatoes would be taken. One of the young boys who had been herding the horses was sent to bring back twenty of the mules they had stolen.

The hundred pound sacks of beans, potatoes and flour were tied on the mules. Two sacks of coffee beans were discovered and a great shout went up. Many of the braves had grown to like coffee. All of the food would be distributed when they got back to their camp.

An hour later, the raiding party was ready to move. Fox Paw stood over the white woman. He had satisfied himself three times with her. More than a dozen braves had emptied their loins in her and pushed themselves back in their breechclouts.

Fox Paw decided the white woman would be more bother than good as a slave. She had fainted several times as the braves used her. She was weak. Now she screamed at him, lunged upward until she pulled free one stake holding her hand. She raked broken fingernails down Fox Paw's chest drawing blood.

Fox Paw swung his knife, slicing her

breast. She screamed and fell back to the ground. Her eyes pleaded with him. Fox Paw shrugged, and swung his sharp knife again, slitting her throat. As she died, he took her scalp. Fox Paw let out a Comanche war cry as the long blonde hair and scalp made a popping noise as it came free. He tied the blonde hair on his lance, and lifted it high.

Every Pony Soldier had been scalped. They had been sliced and cut, mutilated so they could not fight well in the afterlife.

White Eagle made one final check of the wagons. They had left the sacks of sugar, they had no need for them. He had found a strong wooden box, but when he opened it he discovered only worthless yellow discs. They were squaw's clay, too soft to be any good for hunting arrow tips or scrapers. He took three of them, placing them in a leather pouch on his wide leather surcingle. Perhaps Always Smiling would like them.

With a whoop and a shout they rode away with half a dozen army mounts and mules that had survived the attack.

They formed a strange looking war party. Every brave wore some item of clothing from the wagons. Two had on Pony Soldier blue shirts. Several had put on the Cavalrymen's broad brimmed hats with the chin straps.

Half the war lances held fluttering strips of

cloth and freshly taken scalps. One sported a pair of woman's drawers. The warriors shouted and sang as they drove the pack mules across the dry Texas landscape toward a small valley just beyond the sandstone ridge.

There they picked up more than four hundred horses and mules they had stolen on their Texas raids, and began herding the animals west and north toward their lodges high on the headwaters of the mighty Brazos River. The Comanche were safe there.

The small roundeye girl slung across White Eagle's back cried again but White Eagle paid no attention to her. She was safe, she could not get away, and in three days he would give her to Cries In The Morning. She had no children and she had asked him to watch for a small girl to adopt.

White Eagle and his warriors rode toward their camp with happy hearts. It had been a productive raid with many horses stolen. They had not been attacked by any other tribe, had not lost a man, and only four had been wounded by the Pony Soldiers.

The Kwahari Comanches soon would be safely out of the lands penetrated by the roundeyes and back to their wilderness camp where they would always be safe.

Chapter 2

"Five Goddamned days overdue!" Captain Colt Harding thundered at his adjutant. "Five days in that wilderness! That means damn big trouble out here!" The big Cavalryman scoured his hand over his bearded face and slammed his palm down hard on the desk top.

His face showed an angry flush on his cheeks not covered by a dark, close-trimmed beard and his eyes showered his adjutant across his desk with sparks of fury.

"We sent Sergeant Bowers, an old hand with the troop and with the Comanches. He took his fourteen men on a two day ride to meet the wagon train."

Captain Harding swung to the map on the wall of Western Texas. His hand stabbed at Fort Comfort on the White River west of Austin a hundred and twenty miles.

"The escort left us here and were to ride sixty miles to the old Indian Springs camp for the meeting. Then at twelve miles a day, the wagons should have been back here in five days. Seven days overall."

"Yes sir, but those big Pittsburgh freight

rigs can have troubles," First Lieutenant John Riddle said. "Sir, have you ever tried to change a wheel with five thousand pounds of freight pressing it into the sand?"

Captain Harding gave no indication that he had heard.

"It's been twelve days. They are five days overdue." He stood, a man of just over six feet, taller than most men, lean, well muscled and in the best physical condition of his life.

"Call out Troop A, full field gear and rations for five days. No wagons. Issue every man a hundred and twenty rounds. Lieutenant Riddle, I'll lead the patrol. We'll leave in an hour, that'll be at four P.M. You'll remain here in command."

"Yes sir." Lieutenant Riddle gave his commander one last look, then went out the door, through the First Sergeant's office and into the parade ground.

Damn curious, but five days delay out there was not all that unusual, especially for those bastard Pittsburgh freight wagons. He'd done enough supply runs battling the freighters when he was a second lieutenant to last him the rest of his life.

He gave the order to Lieutenant Oliver, CO of A company and Sergeant Casemore, who was with him. They scurried off to get the troops into action.

Riddle looked over the layout of Fort Comfort. It was anything but comfortable. The fort was still being built. After a year it was a little over three quarters finished.

Adobe. It was sturdy, long lasting, but smelled, and it took too long to form the bricks and let them dry in the sun. But when it was done, Fort Comfort would last for a hundred years, long after it was needed he was sure the way the settlers were crowding and pushing each other West all the time.

He heard the whistles shrilling and knew the men were being informed of the patrol. There would be a full company out, ninety-five men and animals. They had nearly an hour to get ready to ride. No small band of Comanches would surprise this patrol.

For the first time, Lieutenant Riddle let his thoughts go to what might have happened to the supply train. The goods were not all that important. But every man on the post knew that the captain's wife and two children were on that supply train. If any harm had come to them, the captain would blow the Comanche apart, one way or the other, with or without official orders.

Even now Captain Harding was splitting his troops in half. Not that they expected any attacks on the fort by the Comanche. The hostiles were still in the raid and retreat mode. But they could change that at any time, join forces with other tribes of hostiles and overwhelm most of the forts along the frontier.

As the cabins, ranches and whites moved farther and farther into the sacred, long-time Comanche hunting grounds, the Indians would probably alter their attacks.

Riddle stood outside the door of the fort's headquarters office. He could hear the men getting ready across the square in the enlisted men's quarters. Fort Comfort would be in the form of a large square when completed. Three of the sides were done, built of tough, durable native Texas mud-clay and straw bricks the Texans called adobe.

The bricks were made in wooden forms twelve by eighteen inches long and four inches thick. They were laid up with adobe mortar in a wall two feet thick that would reject a five inch cannon ball.

Inside the walls were one foot thick with timbers spanning the 24-foot wide rooms. Each side of the square was a little over three hundred feet long. The roofs consisted of tarpaper over the log beams, a foot thick layer of soil on top of the paper and that covered with native sod. The outside wall was usually three feet higher than the roof to afford the troopers a parapet to fire over if they needed to.

Only one corner of the fort quad remained to be done. It would house the future sutter's store, the tack room, and fort smithy, as well as the inside stables. Now the mounts were in the paddock with a sturdy four strand barbed wire fence just in back of where the stables would be, and along the rear of the dependents and guests quarters area.

The captain's orderly came running from the commander's office and hurried to the paddock to ready the captain's horse. He was back quickly, with the big black saddled, the shoes checked, blanket roll in place and the captain's Spencer 7-shot repeater rifle in the boot.

Riddle wished he could get the Spencers for all of his men. They had seven different makes of rifles in the troop. From the old Gallager .52 caliber carbines, to the officers' Spencers, to the Sharps single shot .50 caliber rifle. The Sharps were far too long to be carried on a horse, but they had to use what they had.

At least Riddle had made sure that as many men in each squad had the same caliber and make of weapon as possible. This meant they could share ammunition if needed.

Captain Harding stomped out of his office.

"Ready?" he demanded. His square cut

face was set in a scowl. Heavy brows shading his brown eyes that were guarded but angry at the same time. He wore his battered patrol hat that had an arrow slice through the crown and a bullet hole in the brim. A non-issue gunbelt circled his hips and held two colt .44's with ivory grips. Just in front of the left pistol hung a 12-inch Bowie fighting knife.

"No sir, the men have twenty minutes yet. You did want Lieutenant Oliver to go with you?"

Captain Harding nodded. "I hope someday before I die we get a full complement of officers on this post. We're still short four?"

'Three, Captain. Doctor Jenkins came in last month."

"Yes." Captain Harding stared to the east a moment, then looked back at Riddle. "Keep the usual guards out, no patrols, no wood gathering, all civilians kept inside the walls. We'll force march to the rendezvous if we have to go that far."

He turned away. "Riddle, I . . . I have a bad feeling about this patrol. There's a good chance . . ." He stopped and looked away again. "If we find any evidence of hostiles, we'll pool our provisions, send a tracking squad after them and return for supplies before we follow in force."

"Yes sir," Riddle said. A chill hit him and

he caught the mood the captain was in. He expected the worst. If a wandering party of Comanche had raided the wagon train, or had it pinned down, it would lead to a tremendous confrontation with the hostiles – sooner or later.

If Mrs. Harding was touched or harmed, there would be old Billy Hell to pay in spades.

Captain Harding went back into the office that was adjacent to his quarters. For a long time he looked at a picture of his wife on the dresser. He slipped the tintype from the frame and put it in his blouse pocket, then went back to his office. For a moment he read a communication that had come by messenger from the Military Division of the Missouri in Chicago. He started to read it but put it down.

Nothing mattered now. No orders, no Division demands, no pleas from the settlers. He had to make sure that his wife and children were safe! The Army of the United States had guaranteed them safety!

So where were they?

He checked his pocket watch. One minute to four. He hurried out, saw his orderly with his mount at the step. The lad, Corporal Swenson, sat on his own mount with the double provision bags lashed to his saddle.

Captain Harding stepped into his leather, took a quick report from Oliver who had his men at parade front, and told him to follow.

Behind him Captain Harding heard the familiar orders of: by two's to the left, Hoooo! The ninety-five men swung in behind the captain and his orderly as they rode through the front gate and took the trail east toward Indian Springs.

The captain muttered a small prayer that he would find everyone safe, then checked behind him as Oliver sent out three men as a scouting point and an outrider on each side.

Captain Harding had been over it again and again. Fifteen hours in the saddle would bring them to Indian Springs. He knew in his heart that they would not have to go that far.

They rode for three hours without stopping. Twelve miles, Captain Harding estimated. More than a day's journey for the heavy freight wagons, even along the easy trail through the Texas plains. He told Lieutenant Garland Oliver to give the men a ten minute break for a quick supper. Then they would ride again.

It was a little before ten that night that a lead scout rode back to the column. He went straight to the captain, his face still showing his shock and anger.

"We've found the wagons sir," the private blurted. "A mile ahead. Indians I'm afraid sir! The savages are gone."

Harding spurred his big black forward, nearly unseated the private, brushed past him and charged down the dim trail eastward. Oliver looked at the scout.

"Anyone alive, Private?" he asked.

"No sir. All dead ... and scalped."

"Bring up the troops at a walk, Sergeant Casemore," Oliver shouted, then touched his horse with his knees and pounded down the trail after his commander.

The full moon cast eerie shadows over the scene. Death lay everywhere. Horses hung dead by their reins still tied to the wagon wheels. The fifteen Cavalrymen lay where they had fallen, some under the wagons, some in the open.

Each one had been scalped and sliced with sharp knives. Lieutenant Oliver rode slowly around the scene trying to envision what had happened. When he found the captain's horse, the reins hung down. Colt Harding knelt on the ground behind the last wagon. A form on the ground beside him was still spread eagled and staked to the ground.

"My God!" Oliver whispered. The figure was a woman, naked, her throat slashed, one breast almost cut off. Gently Colt Harding cut the leather bindings that held her to the ground. He picked her up and put his arms around her and rocked back and forth.

Oliver didn't approach him. Instead he found the other two members of the patrol point and told them to build a fire away from the wagons. Then Oliver examined the freight rigs. All the mules pulling the rigs had been killed or stolen. They would need to send for teams. Half the goods were gone or ruined. Still they would need to take all four rigs back to the fort.

He found the broken strong box in the second wagon. It had been smashed open and inside he caught the glint of freshly minted double eagles. His eyes widened. He had never seen so much money in his life. He guessed there was ten thousand dollars worth of gold in the box. He closed it and stood there a moment thinking what he could do with that much money.

The savages could have taken it.

He could bury the box, gold and all and come back...

He could bury the gold, leave the empty box, and let the army think the Comanches had taken the gold.

Oliver hesitated only a second. He was a man to grab any opportunity that came his way. He had maybe ten minutes before the rest of the troops arrived. He used a shovel from the wagon, found a rock outcropping and dug a foot deep hole. He emptied the box of gold double eagles into the hole, covered it and scattered leaves and grass over the spot, then carried the box back to the wagon.

He put the shovel on the wagon. In the morning, with the daylight, he would memorize the exact location of his own private gold mine!

When the troops arrived he ordered them to stay away from the wagons, set them to digging sixteen graves, field depth, three feet. The men groused, but went to work. Every fourth man was required to carry a short shovel.

He sent others to get the longer handled shovels off the wagons.

Oliver made sure Sergeant Casemore had the men working, then went back to the last wagon. Captain Harding had found some of his wife's clothing, and dressed her, forcing stiffening limbs into place. When she was properly covered, he searched the moonlit scene for his children.

In the last wagon he found Yale, and his scream stabbed through the silent Texas night like a dagger. The troops stopped talking and listened. Oliver walked slowly to the wagon and looked in.

In the moonlight streaming through the cut up wagon top he saw Harding kneeling on the bare wooden floor. He held his son in his arms. After several minutes he stood and carried the boy outside and placed him tenderly beside his mother.

Then he went from one of the Cavalrymen to another, checking them, finding each dead. He turned to Oliver who had followed him.

"Sir, we have graves being dug for the troopers."

Harding nodded. "Bury them tonight, you read one service for them all. Then I want every man over here to walk this area foot by foot. I can't find my baby girl, Sadie."

As he said it, Colt Harding sank to the ground, his head went to his hands and he sobbed.

Company A, Second Cavalry, searched a ten acre area around the massacre scene at Buffalo Creek. Nobody found any evidence of little Sadie. Neither did any of the Cavalrymen notice the spot where Garland Oliver had buried the gold. At last the captain called a halt.

Nobody said out loud what he was thinking. If there was no body, the baby girl must be a captive. The Comanches liked to steal young boys and girls, adopt them into families and raise them as Comanches. It happened more often than any of them wanted to admit.

"Unhitch the dead mules from the covered wagons and drag them out of the way," Captain Harding ordered. "Find six horses you can hitch to it, and take it and most of the men back to the fort. Hold a service in the morning for Milly and Yale."

He stared at them in the moonlight. "Men, I want twenty volunteers, all blooded veterans, to go with me following the hostiles' tracks. We'll leave tonight."

He turned to Oliver. "Take four days rations from those men going back to the fort. Divide the rations among the twenty volunteers. That will give us rations enough for sixteen extra days, twenty-one days in all. We'll pursue the killers until we determine their location or direction of travel."

"Yes sir," Oliver said. "You'll start at sunup?"

"No, Lieutenant. You have an hour to find the volunteers, collect the rations and re-distribute them. We'll be moving out at midnight."

Oliver passed the orders. Sergeants took care of finding the volunteers. There was no shortage of them. Many of the soldiers from Company A knew the dead men.

Oliver reported to the captain who sat his

horse looking at the grave sites.

"Sir, after the funeral, I'll return in the morning, with fresh men from B Company, with mules to bring the freight wagons to Fort Comfort. We could leave a guard detail here to protect the Government property."

Captain Harding nodded. "Whatever you decide, Lieutenant."

Promptly at midnight the twenty men and Captain Harding rode away from the death scene. They walked their mounts through the moonlight a half mile to the west, then began a wide circle around the death scene to cut the Indians' trail. Their route took them over the sandstone ridge and down into the small valley beyond.

"They must have eighteen to twenty horses and mules to drive home, as well as any horses they stole on their raiding," Captain Harding said to Sergeant Casemore. The sergeant had been the first volunteer.

"Yes sir. They also could have a hundred head of stolen stock. If we can't find a trail like that in the moonlight, we should go back to Washington D.C. and stand guard duty on the pavement."

They rode side by side, ten yards apart in a troop front formation to sweep a two hundred yard path through the prairie. Halfway through the valley they found where the grass had been trampled and grazed by a large herd of stock or buffalo.

Casemore dismounted and studied the tracks by the light of a torch of burning grass.

"Horses all right, sir. Half of them at least are shod. Hoof prints all over the place. Now all we have to do is see which direction they move."

"West," Captain Harding said. "West into the Staked Plains. Three or four bands of Comanche bands live up there on the high plateau. We've chased them this direction before."

It took them a mile to work out the system. Casemore had been on night tracking trips before. He had found a coal oil lantern among the weapons before they left and had a trooper carry it just in case. Now he lit the lantern and rode ahead a hundred yards and held the light to make sure the tracks were still there.

In some places it was obvious where the large herd had to be driven and they would ride for half a mile before checking the tracks.

Here and there they could see what looked like a strip of land heading west that had been ploughed up by a thousand sharp hooves. Five hundred head of horses and mules would make an easy to follow trail, even at night.

As they moved steadily west, Casemore decided there were more like three hundred head of stock and Indians making the trip.

At times he dismounted and examined the tracks. Every time the blades of grass that had been bent flat to the earth by the hooves had been bruised and scratched, but now had risen back to nearly vertical.

That meant the Indians were at least twelve hours ahead of them. The horse droppings were cold, which told the sergeant about the same thing.

They stopped at three A.M. to brew coffee and chew on hardtack biscuits. The coffee was black, strong and scalding. Casemore realized that his captain had said very little since they started the tracking. He had never seen Captain Harding so remote, so detached, as if he were holding everything inside. It seemed that he couldn't start talking because he might never stop.

The shock of losing a family was terrible, especially when his wife had been naked and spread eagled and used by the savages before she was killed. Garland Oliver had seen the results of Comanche raids before.

They had stopped near a small creek that still had water and filled their individual canteens and the squad, gallon-sized, canvas water bottles.

Casemore studied his big pocket watch in the light of the fire. It had been twenty-eight minutes since they stopped. The captain had given them a half hour. Casemore walked over to where the captain and his orderly sat by their fire.

The orderly held up his hand, palm out. Casemore stopped. The orderly tiptoed away from the fire.

"He's sleeping, Sergeant. I don't think we should wake him."

Sergeant Casemore motioned the orderly back to the fire, and came up humming a song and kicking brush. The captain was awake when the sergeant arrived.

"Sir, this might be a good time to give the men four hours of sleep. We could sack out now and have reveille at 7:30. I think we'll do much better tomorrow with some shuteye now."

Captain Harding had been dreaming about the first time he ever saw his wife back in Connecticut. He shifted by the fire and nodded. "Yes, Sergeant. Order the men down. We'll sleep until 8:30, then ride until dark."

"Yes sir."

They were out there, the savages, the monsters who had desecrated his wife and murdered his son, and stolen his baby daughter. Damn them! He would see them all in the sights of his rifle before he rested. Every damn one of them!

Corporal Swenson walked up with two blankets from the captain's roll. "Your blankets, sir. Shall I keep the fire going?"

"No need, Swenson, get some sleep. We'll have a hard day tomorrow."

Captain Harding lay down and watched the dying fire. Tomorrow they would push it to six miles an hour. Driving even two hundred horses meant the Comanches couldn't make more than three miles an hour at the most.

The raiders were twelve hours ahead . . . maybe thirty miles. A ten hour day at six miles an hour . . . If they could maintain it. He turned over on the hard ground but didn't feel it. Tears stung his eyes. He would never see Milly again, never hold her, never even touch her!

Captain Harding turned away from the fire and stared west. He had one purpose in life now, to avenge his wife and son's deaths and to find his daughter. Little Sadie. Poor, sweet little Sadie!

It took him an hour to fall asleep.

Chapter 3

When White Eagle and his raiders were a mile from their camp on a small tributary of the far reaches of the Brazos River, they stopped and prepared to enter. White Eagle had sent one of the herder boys ahead to tell the People they were back. There would be preparations to make in camp as well.

It was tradition, it was a ritual, it was their culture, recalling the way the Comanche had lived for hundreds of years on the high and the low plains of Texas.

When the messenger arrived, the whole camp burst into an uproar. The women and girls frantically put on their best dresses of chewed antelope and deerskin, those with the fancy trade beads and others with small bells. They greased their hair and combed and braided it and hurried to the far end of the camp where the riders would enter for the grand procession.

The warriors had donned their war paint and some painted their faces black. They tied the fresh scalps high on the end of their lances and attached streamers and ribbons stolen in the raids, and then followed behind Walking

White Eagle as he walked the victorious warriors into camp. There were twenty warriors and almost three hundred horses and mules they had captured. The herd boys drove the heavily laden mules into the center of the camp, but nobody tried to unload them.

The women and girls sang songs of past victories and raids and ran to meet the warriors. Always Smiling, White Eagle's number one wife, carried a long, just peeled sapling that would be the scalp pole where the scalps would be tied for the dance later.

The warriors rode into camp with their lances held high, scalps dangling from them, including one with long blonde hair. Again some of the braves wore items of clothing taken in their raids. The People cheered and shouted as the lances with feathers and streamers were lifted again and again.

Some of the warriors held their shields with long black scalps tied to them. Four of the men were bandaged, but rode with great dignity through the camp of fifty lodges along the stream from one end to the other.

As they came back, each warrior turned off at his own lodge, and gave his wife his fourteen foot lance and shield. They were placed in the spot of honor just outside the door of the lodge. The shield was set on a tripod so it faced the afternoon sun. The long lance leaned against the tripod as well and the warrior's quiver of arrows hung beside it.

The fresh scalps would be quickly readied for the ceremony. Each would be delicately scraped and shaved to remove all of the flesh from inside the scalp skin. Then they would stretch the circle of the scalp over a freshly made willow hoop. Next came the sewing, working from east to south then west to north and back to east. It was the exact way they entered a lodge. The brave would oil the hair and comb it, then attach it to a pole where it would dry all day before it was hung with the older scalps on the freshly cut scalp pole.

The whole camp was alive with talk and joy and activity. Old men sat around in small groups in front of their lodges telling half forgotten tales of their exploits in their younger days. The daring and the feats increased with each telling.

The younger warriors rehearsed the stories of their own coups, acting them out and at times making ear-piercing screams and yells.

The women and girls dug out their best dresses of soft suede leather, and some quickly sewed on more rows of white elk's teeth as decorations. The shiny white teeth were stitched on so they would rattle together as the person walked or danced.

A dance area was cleared in front of White Eagle's lodge. His tipi was the tallest and largest in the whole camp. He needed three wives to take it down, pack it and bundle it on the travois every time they moved ... which was often. His first wife was Always Smiling, a short stern woman who took life seriously and despite her name, seldom smiled. She was as kind as a newborn puppy, and the favorite of the whole camp. She had a dignity and understanding of the medicine bag befitting the chief's wife.

Prairie Flower, twenty-two winters, White Eagle's second wife, was taller and much fatter than Always Smiling. She was a calm person, eager to please, happy to be a chief's wife, and kept hoping to become pregnant again. She had one child, a girl of three. Prairie Flower was the best worker of the group.

Talks A Lot, White Eagle's third wife, was just sixteen, and six months pregnant. She was White Eagle's girl bride, and she had promised him three sons. Less than half of the women in White Eagle's band had children. It was a worry to him. The roundeyes bred like rats with as many as twelve children per house!

Talks A Lot did just that, chattering all the time. She worked alongside the other women, but found little ways to get out of the harder chores. Prairie Flower understood and did much of Talks A Lot's work.

Talks A Lot watched her husband as he sat in front of his lodge beside his shield and lance. Dozens of people came up to congratulate him on his victory, especially over the Pony Soldiers. He showed off his bounty, and gave presents to everyone who came.

He saved only the long yardage of cloth and the ribbons for his wives and the copper kettle. The rest, even his yellow striped blue cavalry pants legs, he gave away. It was his custom to give away all the horses and mules he captured. He had a herd of over a hundred now, and would not trade with the Comancheros until near fall.

He did not give away the rifles and carbines, or the pistols. They were placed in his lodge and would be awarded to braves for special deeds. As raid leader he had asked the men to gather up the rifles, and then claimed them as his own. He would use them to benefit the whole band. The pistols were his without question, and he would present them once he had selected the men to receive them, and trained them how to load and fire them.

The sacks of beans, flour and potatoes were parcelled out to lodges according to need.

White Eagle paid special attention to lodges where widows had no one to support them.

The biggest curiosity of the visitors around White Eagle's lodge was the small roundeye girl who sat on White Eagle's lap. She had long blonde hair and eyes so blue they put the morning sky to shame.

She alternately cringed away from the hands that reached in to touch her and the feel of the Indian man who held her. She had cried at first, but now could cry no more. Her wrists and ankles hurt where she had been tied on the long ride.

They had ridden non-stop after they left the wagons. Twice they changed directions, twice they split into four groups and crisscrossed their trails so even a good Indian tracker would have trouble following them.

Sadie Harding wore the same little blue calico dress she had on when she was captured. The soft blue ribbons were still in her hair. Her long blonde locks were snarled and dirty.

After most of the visitors had left, one thin woman in a worn "best" dress with many rows of elk's teeth sewn on it, came up.

"You had a good raid, White Eagle," Cries In The Morning said. "Many horses and mules, and much of the food of the Pony Soldier. But your greatest prize is there on your knees."

White Eagle smiled. He had known this woman for as long as he could remember. She had one child who died of the great fever, and she needed someone to help her do the work.

"Cries In The Morning, here is my present for you. She has no name yet, but I might suggest one."

Tears showed in the woman's eyes. She could only nod. The child was so beautiful! Like a spring flower in full bloom with her yellow petals and blue eyes.

"We shall call her Laughing Golden Hair. I can see the laughter in her eyes." Chief White Eagle stood and handed Sadie to Cries In The Morning. "I hope you and Running Wolf will want to adopt her."

Again Cries In The Morning nodded as she clutched the startled child to her bosom. It was too much to hope for! So many times she had believed that she was pregnant, but each time she was not. Now she would have a family for Running Wolf, who had chosen not to have another wife. Perhaps now he would feel proud enough to buy a young wife, a strong one with wide hips for easy child birthing!

Cries In The Morning mumbled her hurried thanks and rushed away, the small Laughing Golden Hair child in her arms. She hurried through the camp, nodding and smiling to the other women who looked with surprise and some jealousy to see that she had been given the golden hair.

Cries In The Morning entered her lodge, carefully walked to the left and went around the small fire that glowed in the center fire pit, and then sat on her pallet of buffalo robes and the fox fur and stared at her new child.

"You are so young and will soon forget your old ways and become one of the People," Cries In The Morning crooned. "I will grease your hair and braid it to keep it out of the way, and I will make you a small, proper dress of the finest chewed suede with hundreds of elk's teeth! You will have tiny moccasins all beaded and proper, and a small breechclout made exactly to your size, so your pale white body can slowly tan and turn brown like a pecan nut!"

Cries In The Morning knew the small one did not understand one word of what she was saying. But the soft, gentle hands, her smile, and the clay pot of thick stew from the fire let her know she was going to be treated kindly.

Sadie Harding looked up at this strange woman, who was so thin she seemed about to blow over. She had on a funny looking dress with ugly white teeth on it, and her face was smudged and dirty over her dark brownish red skin. But she smiled. Sadie knew a smile.

"I hate you!" Sadie screeched. "I hate you and I want to go home. My home is Fort Comfort. I want to go there right now!" Sadie crossed her arms, put an angry scowl on her face and refused to eat any of the disgusting smelling food she was offered.

"I hate you and I'm hungry, and I want a cookie!"

Outside the tipi of White Eagle, preparations were continuing for the dance.

In White Eagle's lodge his wives had on their best suede dresses. They took out their favorite brass bracelets and slid them on their arms. Then they braided each other's hair and painted vermillion down the hair part. The last thing they did was to paint one another's faces, and the inside of their ears the same bright red.

Outside the drummers had begun their continual pounding and the singers were wailing and chanting out the traditional songs of the successful raid against the enemy, whether another tribe, the hated People Eaters or the roundeye. It was beginning to get dark outside.

At the dance site, a large council fire had been built in the cleared area. The members of the council sat in a semicircle around the crackling blaze. Each of the leaders of the band wore his robes over his shoulders even though it was still summertime warm.

The scalp pole with all of the new scalps had been planted solidly into the ground in front of them. Prominent was the long yellow hair scalp.

Cries In The Morning had brought Sadie to the dance, even though she wouldn't understand. It was a good time for her to see her first victory dance and hear tales of taking coups.

The dancers were in the open part now. They circled the scalp pole, then divided into two lines, one of men and one of women facing each other. They danced forward until they almost met, then worked backwards to the steady beat of the drums. The costumes and jewelry of the women rattled as they danced.

Then from out of the light of the fire there came a Comanche victory scream and the dancers stopped and crowded back.

Suddenly a rider galloped into the clearing and a warrior, Fox Paw, drove his fourteen-foot lance into a buffalo hide that had been spread out near the council.

The drums stopped and there was total silence around the leaping fire as Fox Paw told of his first coup and then of the taking of the white woman. After he had dramatized his coups, he dismounted and joined the other warriors near the council.

Before the People could start talking, another warrior raced in and gave his account of his coups on the raid.

Cries In The Morning held her new child on her lap where she sat at the edge of the firelight. She wanted the small one to see everything, so she would understand it.

"The braves are telling the council about how brave they were in battle and on the raid against the Pony Soldiers. Later the council will sort out the claims and award the coups to each man. No warrior can get credit for more than two coups from any one enemy."

Cries In The Morning explained each of the steps as the warriors rode in, realizing that the small white child did not understand the words, but it was a beginning. It was like having a new baby who was four winters old, but could not speak yet or understand the language of the People.

Sadie looked at this strange woman and scowled.

"It's not so hard to understand, Laughing Golden Hair," Cries In The Morning explained. "It doesn't matter which warrior has the scalp. It shows much more bravery to strike a live enemy with a coup stick than to lift the scalp off a dead enemy, but another brave can count coup on him as well, perhaps before he was dead. Battles are always confusing, but the council sorts it all out to determine who really earned the coups."

The tales of coup taking went on into the night until every brave had driven his lance into the buffalo skin and the tales were told. Then there was more dancing that went on for as long as any of the revelers could stand.

There was no stupid water in the Eagle Band camp. White Eagle had seen what the white man's fire water did to the Indian who drank it. Whenever they found whiskey or rum in their raiding, the kegs or casks were opened and drained or the bottles broken. No brave in the Eagle Band would violate the unwritten law of their leader.

Long before the last coup story had been told, Laughing Golden Hair had slumped asleep against the dry, sagging breasts of Cries In The Morning. She smiled softly, her eyes showing the great love she had built so fast for the small, helpless roundeye with the golden halo around her head. Cries In The Morning knew that she had a lifelong job of teaching the small golden one of the ways of the Comanche, so some day she could marry a great chief, and help lead their people.

Cries In The Morning carried her small

charge tenderly as she went back to her lodge, entered and put Sadie down in the bed of buffalo robes and soft fox pelts, so she would have a thick mattress and stay warm during the cool of the evening.

Gold Eagle and the council worked out the conflicting coups and awarded them to the warriors. When that was done Walking White Eagle went to his lodge and put down the entrance flap so no one would come in. He was finished for the evening.

He dug out the three round pieces of squaw's clay from the small bag tied to his surcingle and gave one of them to each of his wives. Always Smiling looked at it, bit it and left tooth marks, she shrugged and thanked White Eagle, but he knew she would soon trade it to Prairie Flower for ribbon. Each of them received the ribbons he had saved and the long piece of cloth.

Prairie Flower smiled when he gave her the roundeye's gold double eagle. She began boring a hole in it with a sharpened piece of metal she was making for a lance point. Soon she had the hole and she threaded a tough piece of buffalo sinew through it to make a necklace.

Talks A Lot watched with nervous excitement as White Eagle came to her. When he gave her the coin she squealed in delight and stroked his chest showing her appreciation. She at once began bargaining with Prairie Flower.

White Eagle sat on a buffalo robe near the small fire, watching the twigs burn, turn to ash and then wither into nothing but hot air and smoke.

It was the way of all life, he thought. Here on Mother Earth for only a few years, then to die and wither and turn to dust and bones, while Mother Earth went on for many hundreds of winters. She watered her hair and trees, kept the berries and nuts growing and brought the buffalo in the thousands over the prairies to feed and clothe the People.

Now the whites, the roundeyes came. When he was a boy, the roundeyes stayed far to the east, away from Comanche hunting grounds. They seldom saw the white men. But now they came farther and farther into the land the People had shared with Mother Earth for hundred of winters.

Why couldn't the Pony Soldiers stay to the east, and out of the sacred lands of the Comanche? He shook his head. He would never understand the whites. Never.

He felt a need. Perhaps his medicine would be strong tonight and he could sire a son. He went to Prairie Flower where she lay in her robes near their small daugher. White Eagle's hand went under the buffalo robe and stroked her soft, small breasts. She sat up at once and welcomed him.

"Tonight I will make you a son," she whispered in his ear as they lay down under the robes. It was the dream they both longed for, but after three years it had not happened.

Perhaps tonight, he thought as he moved over her and she opened herself to him.

Early the next morning, just as the sun broke over the far flat horizon, White Eagle lifted from the robes, dressed quickly and walked to the upstream end of the camp where most of his horses and ponies were pastured.

Two sleepy herder boys who had been standing watch all night saw him and waved in greeting. Soon the daytime herders would come to watch the precious stock. A warrior's wealth was measured by the number of horses he could steal and how many wives he could afford.

White Eagle had lost his favorite war pony on the last raid. One of the Pony Soldiers had shot the fleet gray from under him, and he had scrambled to find another before the raid was over. White Eagle had screamed in rage when his war pony went down. To a Comanche warrior his war pony was his most prized and most important possession, far outstripping the value of his wives and children.

A warrior was nothing without a good war pony. A Comanche brave cheerfully and without thought loaned his wife to a friend. He could expect the favor in return. A warrior risked his life for his friends and brothers without a moment's hesitation.

But he would share or give his war pony to no man.

He would guard the life of his war pony over that of most of his friends and relatives. He would not let a good war pony slip from his hands, not unless he were mortally wounded.

But the Pony soldiers had snatched Devil Wind away from him. Now he would have to train a second war pony. Every warrior had a second pony in training. But with White Eagle's second mount, there was much work to be done.

He called out to Flying Wind, then whistled. The two year old stallion whinnied and left the herd and trotted up to where White Eagle stood. At least that training had been completed. White Eagle rubbed the mount's head and ears, gave him a handful of grass that he especially liked and then steadied him while he put on a surcingle, this one a four inch wide band of braided strips of leather that circled Flying Wind's back and belly.

The pony stood still. He was used to the cinch, used to being ridden, but the exacting training for a war pony was far from over. A Comanche brave had to be able to ride without using his hands, which he kept for shooting his bow and rifle, and for attacking with his lance. The smallest pressure by the rider's knees, legs, feet had exact meanings the war pony must know and respond to instantly.

The best trained ponies told, with the movements of their ear, their riders of the approach of other riders and if they were friend or foe. The war pony, when properly trained, would put the best Western cutting quarter horse to shame. White Eagle sat on a ridge all day once watching the roundeye cowboys below working with the stock.

A war pony could have done the cutting job in half the time. The Texas cattle were plodding and slow compared to the shaggy buffalo which any war pony had to be able to outrun, outmaneuver and out think.

White Eagle knew Flying Wind had the ability, he was like his father in many ways. Now he mounted the young gray which had spots of black from his mother, and rode easily for five minutes. Then he headed across a small meadow at a gallop.

Flying Wind accepted the challenge and stopped only when White Eagle pulled back sharply on a braided hair hackamore and ground his toes into the horse's ribs at the same time.

He made the stop ten times, and the last time Flying Wind stopped abruptly when only the toe pressure was applied.

White Eagle praised the big gray and went on to a new lesson. He charged straight at a two-foot thick maple tree. Six feet before he would have slammed into the tree, Flying Wind veered around it.

The second time White Eagle raced the war pony at the tree and touched him with his toes at the last moment and the big gray slid to a stop within inches of the tree. Three more times they did the same routine.

The next time White Eagle touched his left knee to the mount's flank and pulled the hackamore to the right turning him around the tree on the right.

Over and over and over, White Eagle repeated the instruction, until Flying Wind would respond quickly and deliberately to the learned commands.

After two hours White Eagle rubbed down his mount with hands full of fresh grass, removing all sign of sweat and lather, then led him along the creek to drink and higher to a favorite spot filled with thistles that the horse loved.

Back at the pasture, he checked his other stock from Flying Wind's back, decided he would keep the next batch of horses and mules he stole so he would have a hundred for trading with the Comancheros, the Mexican traders who ventured far into the Comanche hunting grounds once a year loaded with many goods that the Indians wanted and could pay for with horses.

Back at the camp, White Eagle stopped at Cries In The Morning to see how the small child was doing. He knew that Running Wolf would show little interest in the child. That was woman's work. Besides, she was a roundeye and while he had agreed to adopt her, he would have rather had a child of his loins.

White Eagle saw the pair outside the lodge. Cries In The Morning was radiant. She sat with her metal scraper, working on a buffalo hide. Beside her, Laughing Golden Hair held a small scraper with both hands and tried to do the same work. Cries In The Morning laughed and helped her, giving approval when she did it right.

White Eagle watched for a few moments more, heard the woman patiently teaching the child words of the Comanche tongue. Yes, it would be all right. The small roundeye would soon learn the language, and grow and learn the ways of the People. In two years Laughing Golden Hair would be a Comanche forever.

Chapter 4

The troops of the Second Cavalry rolled out of their blankets the next morning promptly at 8:30 to the sounds of the bugler's reveille. Sergeant Casemore wondered how far the notes of the trumpet would carry in the open country, a mile? five miles? It might be good not to use the bugle on routine calls on this patrol.

He made sure every man ate a hearty breakfast of coffee, beans and hardtack. It would be their last hot meal for some time, the sergeant guessed. He'd never seen the old man so angry, so silent, and deadly furious. There was going to be hell to pay, and Casemore was glad he was on Captain Harding's side.

He reported to the commander's small A style tent. It was the same size shelter the troopers used. The only difference was he slept in his alone. The bugler and the captain's orderly shared a second A tent nearby.

Captain Harding had finished his own hot beans and coffee and was munching on some sweet rolls he had brought along. He had his shot-up campaign hat on. That always meant he was ready for battle.

"Sir, the patrol is ready to form up on your command," Casemore reported. "All men and mounts are present and accounted for." He saluted smartly. Captain Colt Harding, usually one for strict military courtesy, half saluted, half waved in response.

"Five minutes, Sergeant. Wished to hell we'd brought along some of those Tonkawa scouts. Put your best tracker out a half mile in front of us with two men in a connecting file. One man to ride sweep on each side at two hundred yards. We'll move out as soon as you get your assignments made."

"Yes sir!" Casemore said snapping another salute. He did a proper about face and trotted back to the troopers thirty yards down a slight slope.

Three hours later they were still making what Captain Harding figured was about five and a half miles an hour. He walked the troop most of the time, but gave the mounts a ground eating lope for ten minutes out of every hour.

The trackers had no trouble following the wide trail. They functioned more as forward scouts than trackers. The youngest recruit in the patrol could see the path the big herd of horses had cut through the short plains grasses.

At noon on the first day they found a spot where the herd had paused long enough to drink and graze for "about an hour" the trackers reported. Then the horses were split into eight groups and driven off in eight different directions. All the trails still headed generally north and west.

The scout, a civilian called Hatchet, waited for the main party at the division of the trails.

Harding took the report of the scout and stared at the countryside for a moment. To the far north he could see the start of a few higher ridges.

"The Concho River up that way?" he asked. "A tributary to the Colorado?"

The scout nodded. "Another fifty, sixty miles, maybe more. Gets a little higher but not much."

The captain scowled. "Figures, this is Texas. We'll take a compass bearing of northwest, and follow whichever trail leads closest to that. This is some kind of trick, trying to confuse us. We hang together and we move fast. Lead scout, half mile ahead, otherwise same information." The captain nodded at Sergeant Casemore who whipped his mount around and bellowed at the troops.

"Detail! By two's, left wheel into column! March!"

The troops moved out behind the captain and sergeant. They rode at a canter for half a mile, then dropped to a walk.

An hour later they left the small stream they had been near and the tracks broke across a broad stretch of flat prairie with nothing to be seen for miles except the shimmering heat of the day on the sparse dirt and sand.

Hatchet came back from the point.

"Sir, we just found two tracks joining this one, looks like they are coming back together for the final march."

Captain Harding set his jaw a little firmer. "How far behind them are we?"

"Can't understand it. We're losing ground, sir. Figure the hostiles are now more than eighteen hours ahead of us."

Harding took off his weathered campaign hat and wiped sweat from his forehead. He looked at Casemore.

"Why, Sergeant?"

"We're pushing big army mounts, sir,

which are pampered and grain fed. Those Comanches got their war ponies under them, and on the run back to their lodges. They trade horses, I'd wager. Ride one for six months, then switch to a fresh one for six. They must have been riding steady for at least thirty-six hours to be that far ahead."

"It's possible to push their stock that hard?"

"Yes sir. Seen it done before. The Comanche use grass fed ponies, tough little animals that are sturdy and hardy. They'll ride them for six hours twice as fast as we can push ours. Happens."

"So we can't catch them?"

"Not a round-balled chance in hell, sir."

"But we can track them! We move out at our usual pace. They've got to stop sooner or later, and we've still got twenty days of rations. Let's move, Sergeant Casemore!"

"Yes sir!" Casemore wheeled his big black, barked orders and the column swung out again to the northwest. They found the added tracks and another mile on the whole herd seemed to be trampling down the prairie grass.

After ten more miles they came to a spot where the herd had grazed.

"Here about two hours," Hatchet, the scout, said. "Still sixteen hours out in front of us, at least."

There was no dinner break. The men ate in their saddles, groaning and grousing.

"Shut up, you assholes!" Casemore bellowed at them. "At least the Comanche aren't slicing your guts open the way they did that escort party. Consider yourselves lucky!"

They rode all afternoon.

By a little after 5:30 the scout came back reporting the first signs of water in more than five hours.

"Small crick, Sergeant, enough water to keep the horses happy. Probably a tributary to the Middle Concho. We're probably too far west to be hitting the southern branch."

When Casemore reported this to the captain, Harding grunted.

"We'll water everything well there, men and stock, then ride five more hours. We can't afford to let that trail get too cold."

At the stream, the men drank first, holding the horses back so they wouldn't roil the water.

Private Victor bellied down by the little stream and gathered a double handful of water to splash in his face. Before he could move, a water moccasin struck from where it lay next to a rotted branch in the stream.

Victor screamed and the trooper beside him brought the heel of his heavy black boot down on the reptile and smashed its head into a flat oozing mass.

"Marlin!" Victor screamed holding his arm. The venom had jetted into his wrist.

Corporal Adolph Marlin was the unofficial medic on marches. He worked with the battalion doctor when he was in the fort. Now he ran up and brought out a short medical knife.

He looked at the twin fang marks.

"Yep, a poisonous bite. Take just a minute." He sliced each of the marks with an "X," applied a small rubber suction cup, then drew out blood and the poison. He squirted the blood on the ground to be sure he had removed enough, then he put some alcohol on the cuts, bandaged them and slapped Victor on the shoulder.

"Good as new. Next time look around before you start drinking. If you'd laid down and stuck out your neck, you could be damn near dead now. Hard to make incision cuts in your throat!"

Captain Colt Harding walked up and down a twenty yard stretch of the creek. He looked northwest. Always he watched that direction. He knew he would see nothing, but he also knew his tiny, beautiful, sweet and tender daughter of four years was still somewhere out there in that direction. She was a captive of the most savage, inhuman, terrible creatures that Colt Harding had ever seen.

He owed them more than they could ever pay. He would have his revenge for the deaths of his beloved Milly and his son Yale, and then he would recapture and free his daughter!

Or he would die trying.

He motioned to Swenson to bring his mount. He swung up and looked northwest again. The land rose slightly, not enough to notice, but it was lifting as they worked toward the Cap Rock Escarpment well north of them.

"If we can't catch them, Corporal, we can damn well track them. We'll find them. We have to find them!"

"Yes sir," Swenson said.

At sunset Hatchet was replaced by the second tracker who took the lantern and worked out a hundred yards at a time, unless he was sure where the herd might go by the landscape. It slowed their net gain, but it helped.

Half the time the troops sat on quiet horses while the tracker found the way.

At 10 P.M. by his pocket watch, Captain Harding gave the word to halt. They had come at last to the middle fork of the Concho River. Here it was no more than a small stream flowing through a wild and treeless land where shrubs and scrub growth dominated what little vegetation there was higher than the grass.

They camped there.

"No fires!" Sergeant Casemore warned each of the groups of men. "Cold food and then into the blankets. We'll be moving early in the morning."

Casemore suggested he take the bugler's mouthpiece to prevent any automatic response by the musician. Captain Harding agreed while the bugler snorted.

Casemore took the first watch with two other men. They would protect the camp until 2 A.M. when the next shift would come on and wake up the troopers at six in the morning.

It was a dry, quiet camp and Captain Harding sat by his saddle. He wondered how Sadie was this night? Was she warm enough? Did they feed her? She had been prone to colds and earaches. He hoped they took care of her.

Colt Harding had not the slightest doubt that he would find and rescue his daughter. A band of savages would be no match for a concentrated, carefully planned attack by even a twenty man patrol of U.S. Cavalrymen.

Holding that thought firmly in hand, Captain Harding went to sleep and did not dream.

Daylight came at five that morning.

Sergeant Casemore sent out the two trackers and a scout to check the trail for a mile, then to bring back a report. The scout was back before the men were roused. Hatchet looked troubled as Casemore saddled his mount.

"Damn Indians split up the herd again, Sarge. Looks like at least twenty groups going off in every damn direction of the compass. I don't know what the hell they're doing."

Casemore pushed the scout out of the way and slapped his mount so she'd let out a bellyful of air so he could cinch up the belly strap.

"They're trying to get home. I've seen them do this before. There just isn't any way to hide twelve hundred sets of hoof prints."

"What the hell you going to tell the captain?"

"Same thing I told you. Get back out there and tell your trackers to move upstream on the Concho River here and see what they find. If nothing after three miles, break it off and meet us back at the split up."

"It's a possibility."

"Damn right. Why come this far and

backtrack? Not a Comanche. Now get moving."

Casemore watched Hatchet move out, then went to see the captain with a report of the latest developments.

By the time the patrol reached the next point where the Comanches had split the herd, the scouts were back from upriver on the Concho.

The scout, a big, rawboned Texan, said he knew every inch of every Texas county, grinned at Casemore.

"By damn! They're coming back together. Some of them must have gone up the river. Found several places they splashed out when they came to deep pools. How'en hell you know they was gonna do that, Casemore?"

"The only way to get twelve years experience fighting Comanches is to fight Comanches for twelve years. Any more stupid questions, Hatchet? Go tell the captain what you found."

The troops moved up to the new juncture point and found five or six trails merging. Then they vanished almost completely.

"Few traces here and there," Hatchet said, a frown in his voice. "Where'n hell them savages go?"

Casemore studied the terrain as the captain came up. Colt Harding looked over the juncture of two tributaries and the partially flooded, swampy area ahead of them. He walked his big black into the soupy wet land then back out. No prints showed.

"You could ride a whole division of Cavalry through here with eight pounders and never leave a track," Harding said. "The bastards are here somewhere. Position the patrol on a searching front and we'll sweep through this mire. Tell the men to watch out for quicksand."

The troopers were brought up in a long skirmish line, spaced five yards apart and they moved ahead at a walk. There was no quicksand, and little firm ground. A quarter of a mile across the large marshy area, they came back to hard earth and stopped.

The scouts found no sign of hoof prints or horseshoe marks on the solid land.

Captain Harding sat on the small rise and looked at the rest of the swamp. It seemed like a half dried up lake that had flooded again, and now was in the process of drying up once more. He followed the contours of the dry land on both sides and slowly swung to the north.

On that end the swamp turned into a heavy woods that seemed to shroud an opening leading to a low ridge farther north. There should be some sort of a valley below the ridge. It was a perfect blind for a concealed opening. They could ride through the swamp, which would wipe out any evidence of passage, through the woods and into the valley.

He rode a dozen yards straight for the woods, motioned for Casemore to line up the troops and they moved toward the pecans and willows and other small hardwoods that clogged the far end of the swampy area.

They were within twenty yards of the screen of trees and brush when one of the troopers screeched in pain and grabbed his shoulder. An Indian arrow quivered there, the steel point slashing through his blouse and into his upper arm.

"First squad, one round into the brush ahead!" Captain Harding ordered. The first squad to his left brought up their weapons. "Fire!"

Eight weapons went off in a roar and leaves and twigs and some branches shivered as the rounds blasted into the woodland.

"Charge!" Harding bellowed and the twenty-three men raced full gallop at the trees, splashing water on each other as the horses surged through the marsh.

There were no more arrows from the woods. The captain was the first rider into the greenery. He slashed through brush and small trees and fifty feet into the growth it thinned to nothing and a small valley opened to a chattering stream dancing down a rocky bed.

A quarter of a mile up the short valley he spotted two Comanches kicking their horses as they raced around a slight bend in the opening and were gone.

There were no campfires here, no evidence that the band had camped here. This was their vanishing point, where they would confuse the stupid roundeyes and force them to go back to their fort.

Harding wanted to chase them, but he knew it was probably a trap to lure them into a crossfire of whistling arrows and point blank rifle fire. Not today, Comanche savages. He held up his hand and his men stopped as they came through the screen of trees.

He ordered them back into the trees for cover, then let Corporal Marlin treat Private Kelly's arrow wound. The metal point had penetrated flesh beyond the prongs but had not gone all the way through the upper arm.

Adolph looked at Kelly who sat on the bank of the stream. They didn't have time to use whiskey, and had had none of the new ether. He moved suddenly, bumping the shaft in Kelly's shoulder.

"Oh, God!" the wounded private roared, then passed out from the pain.

Captain Harding stood nearby watching.

"Sorry, Captain," Marlin said. "It's the only thing I can do. The arrowhead has to come out." He looked at the depth of the arrow. He had to push it on through or dig it out. He figured he'd do less damage digging it out. Marlin used the scalpel from his kit and cut the flesh on both sides of the points until he could pull the arrow back.

Blood spurted. Marlin swore, pushed a white towel over the bleeding and when he tugged the arrow out he bound the towel firmly around the wound. After it stopped bleeding he would try to pull the sides of the wound together so it would not scar so much.

He washed Kelly's face with cold water from the stream and he soon came around groaning with pain and swearing in three languages. He couldn't lift his arm. Marlin made a sling for him from a pair of kerchiefs, then helped him mount and they moved out of the trees, through the marshy area to hard ground.

Captain Harding found a draw where they could camp for the night. He had no thoughts of pushing after the hostiles. Not with only twenty men. He would return to the fort, prepare a proper force and come after the

Comanche with a high percentage chance of raiding their camp and finding his daughter. Now they would rest, put out good security, and let their wounded men gain some strength.

They had a hot meal that evening and fires, and defied the Comanche to come for them. It was a quiet night.

The next morning they kicked into their saddles at 6:30 and moved at a steady four miles per hour, backtracking the trail, cutting across areas where they knew they could, and angling well around the site of the massacre. They could save half a day's travel by moving at a better angle toward the fort.

Three days later after an uneventful return march, they arrived within sight of Fort Comfort. Private Kelly had developed a low fever but had managed to sit his saddle without having to be tied on. He would go directly to the post surgeon's office.

First Lieutenant Riddle met them half a mile from the fort. He rode alongside a quiet Captain Harding.

"Nothing untoward happened during your absence, Captain Harding," Riddle reported. "The funeral services were held as per your instructions."

"Thank you."

"Did you locate the hostiles, sir?"

"We tracked them, found their general site, and have returned to gather a force to face them down." They rode in silence for a time.

"Anything in the dispatch from San Antonio?"

"Nothing unusual. General Sheridan is talking about a new way to rid the west of the Indian. A way to end the Indian wars once and for all. It's quite unusual."

"Right now I have my own Indian war to fight," Captain Harding said. He looked into the distance, and they didn't talk for the rest of the ride into the fort.

They arrived in the afternoon, and it wasn't until the next morning that Riddle broke the bad news to Captain Harding.

"Sir, the bills of lading were found in the material from the wagons. There is some disturbing news."

"Disturbing, Riddle? I don't understand."

"One of the shipments listed was a wooden chest filled with eight thousand dollars worth of gold double eagle coins with the mint date of 1869 stamped on them."

"Yes? So what's your point?"

"A wooden chest was found that had a few gold filings and gold dust in it, however there were no gold coins found. None whatsoever. There is eight thousand dollars in gold missing from the wagons."

Captain Colt Harding stared at his adjutant. "No mistake?"

"I'm afraid not. You know the Comanche, they call gold woman's clay because it's good for nothing but trinkets. Too soft for arrow points, axes or scrapers. The chances of the Indians stealing the gold are almost non-existent."

"Which leaves our greeting party, and the men who brought the wagons back to the fort. All members of my command."

"I'm sorry, Captain. That's the way it looks."

Captain Harding wanted to laugh. He had a real problem, and this insignificant item popped up and took on an inflated importance. They would find the gold. It would be much harder finding Sadie. He'd never find Milly or Yale again.

He slammed his palm down hard on his heavy desk and stood.

"All right. Write up your report. Lay it out exactly as you see it. They'll want to know the exact items stolen or destroyed by the Comanche. Give them line and verse on it. And include the eight thousand dollars in missing gold. We'll let San Antonio bring the charges."

"Going to be bloody hell to pay, Captain,"

Riddle said.

This time Harding did laugh. "Lieutenant, I'm already making all the payments I can to hell. You handle it."

"The paperwork is all done along those lines. I've had a week. If I could have your authorizing signature?"

Captain Harding signed the papers made out with three copies and a rough for their own files.

"I'll send two couriers this evening, as soon as it's dark. The men will leave six hours apart. Each with identical dispatches. One of them should get through. They'll travel only by night until they are well out of Comanche country."

Captain Harding nodded. He stared out his window into the parade ground. "I'll be putting together a long range patrol, Lieutenant. I'll need a hundred men, provisions for thirty days, two supply wagons, and twenty extra horses. We're going to run these bastards to ground and bury them."

He looked up at a knowing stare on his adjutant's face.

"May I go along, sir?"

"No. You've got a fort to run. Get the wheels in motion to put together the force. How many of the Tonkawa Indian scouts do we have on post?"

"About twenty braves, sir."

"Good, I'll take them all. They hate the Comanches, love nothing better than to slice them up. Let's say three hundred rounds per trooper, Riddle. And we'll take the Gatling gun. I want to show these hostiles that we mean business."

"Special order, sir, from Division?"

Captain Harding looked at his second in command for ten seconds without saying a word. They had been friends on this post for almost a year. They got drunk together every Saturday night. They were both married and their wives had been back east.

Colt Harding shook his head. "John, you know we don't have any special orders. We'll be working under standing orders about pursuit of hostiles where civilians or military personal are wounded or killed and civilian or army property is destroyed. It's good enough for General Sheridan, it's good enough for me. Any questions?"

"No, Colt, but I do have a suggestion. Get out of here before some major or light colonel comes flying in here from San Antonio looking for that damned eight thousand in gold!"

Chapter 5

The men of A company's extended patrol had been back for a full day now. Captain Harding paced his office wishing he could get into the field tomorrow.

That wasn't possible. It took several days to get up the supplies, the plans, the personnel and the army's way of doing things to get a two month campaign mounted and ready for the trail.

That didn't make it any easier to handle. Last night at taps, Captain Harding had slipped out to the lonesome graves just beyond the fort where regulations dictated they had to be. There was no grass, no flowers, just two simple wooden crosses with the names painted on them. He had to make better arrangements.

At the common grave he had wept, not caring if anyone saw him. He had loved Milly so deeply, so completely, that he had never even looked at another woman. She was the foundation that kept him sane in this insane world.

He wept for Yale as well. A fine young boy who never had a chance to grow up. That was the real tragedy. The Comanches probably figured he was too old to re-train as an Indian.

Lieutenant Riddle had powered ahead on preparations for the patrol. He was calling it that for the paperwork. There were dozens of details to run down. Rations alone was a problem with fifty headaches attached. There had to be more than beans and hardtack for two months in the field.

Captain Harding had set this morning as time to do a practice run with the Gatling gun. He called for his horse and rode out to the practice range just north of the camp. A smashed wagon had been set up as a target three hundred yards away.

When Lieutenant Oliver saw him coming, the Company A commander rode up and saluted.

"We're about to do our first live round firing practice on the Gatling gun, sir. Would you like to observe?"

"Yes," Harding said, barely holding in his impatience. Why else would he have ridden out here?

They rode to a point where a dozen enlisted men sat on the short plains grass. Oliver raised his arm and brought it down.

A hundred yards to the left a team of horses charged forward pulling a light caisson and a wheel mounted, ten barrel Gatling gun that bumped and jolted over the uneven ground. The driver of the gun rig rode the horse on the right. He wheeled it around in front of the officers so the trailing gun aimed at the target wagon. Two troopers raced up on their mounts, leaped off, unhitched the gun from the caisson and swung it around to aim directly at the target.

The Gatling gun was mounted on smaller wheeled units than the artillery used, but they were the same type. There were a pair of horses that pulled each rig, which consisted of the wheel mounted gun, and a second detachable two wheel caisson with its mounted box used for equipment, cleaning gear and mainly ammunition.

When the double rig stopped, the gunners detached the rear unit, which was the gun itself, from the front half, dropped the trailing hitching mount and positioned the tongue to give the gun a firm foundation. Then the weapon was set to fire.

The gunners made minor adjustments, positioned the trailing leg of the caisson, then adjusted the ammunition supply and the sergeant in charge held up his arm that he was ready to fire.

It was a ten barrel, crank operating Gatling that the manual said could blast out four hundred rounds a minute. Captain Harding knew that in practice it seldom fired half that many because of the barrels fouling by the deposits from the black powder. But even two hundred rounds a minute could be devastating.

Oliver brought his hand down and the sergeant on the gun turned the crank. Each time the ten rifle barrel cylinder turned to a new barrel, a round fired automatically. The faster the crank was turned, the faster the barrels rotated and the faster the weapon fired.

After a dozen rounds the sergeant stopped, adjusted the aim of the weapon and fired again. This time twenty rounds blasted into the side of the wagon and the troops on hand cheered.

The next cranking produced only ten shots when twenty should have come out.

Oliver signalled to cease fire, and rode up to the gun.

The gunners opened the assembly, quickly cleaned the clogged barrels and when ready they fired another twenty rounds.

"That's plenty of practice," Captain Harding barked. Then he shook his head. "No, I want the assistant gunner and the third man on the firing team to be able to operate the weapon as well as the gunnery sergeant. If the sergeant becomes a casualty, the other men must be able to fire. Both you other men practice firing twenty rounds. Move the weapon, re-aim and fire it. See to it, Lieutenant Oliver." The captain returned the officer's salute and then rode back to the fort.

On his desk he found notes from the only two officers' wives on the post. Each invited him to dinner, one that night, the other the next night. He sighed and stared at the wall map without seeing it. The women were only trying to compensate, to make his loss easier.

But he wasn't ready to be civil or polite, not yet. He had revenge in his heart first. When the bloody Comanche band was run to ground and every man slaughtered, only then would he feel clean enough to associate with respectable families. Only then would he be able to enjoy seeing a family together, while his own had been murdered and kidnapped.

He took a deep breath, beat down the grinding ache in his gut and wiped his hand across his eyes. Then he called in his clerk and orderly.

"Corporal Swenson, take my regards to Mrs. Edwards and to Mrs. Jenkins. I won't be able to accept their kind offers to dinner. Pressing work getting ready for the patrol. Say something nice. Thank you, Corporal."

Swenson watched the captain a moment,

started to say something then nodded and retreated to his small office outside the door.

Captain Harding went back to the map on his wall and studied the trail from Fort Comfort north and west to the middle fork of the Brazos. He knew the trail, it was embedded in his brain. He estimated the days. With the wagons, at least six long days to the marshy area and the hidden canyon.

What he would do once he got to the canyon, he wasn't sure. A plan of action kept surging through his mind, but he couldn't formulate anything solid yet. He had to wait and see what his scouts reported.

This time he'd take the Indians, the Tonkawa. They hated the Comanche as much as he did. A good fight would help keep them happy.

He dug into his files and took out a paper he had written almost a year ago about how to settle the Indian question once and for all. It was war, and they should take a war stance. They could not chase all over a billion square miles hunting the renegades – and finding them only when they wanted to fight.

What the army had to do was strike at the Indian camps, at the very heart of the Indian villages, the base camps, the squaws and their tents and racks of drying meat, their winter food stores.

The Indians must be treated the same way they treated the whites, kill everyone at the villages, burn down and totally destroy everything they owned.

The way the Comanche had done at the wagon supply train!

Captain Harding took out the paper now and read it again. Yes, it was practical. It was the only way to defeat the threat to the white settlers. The army had to destroy the Indian's way of life so he could not function independently. So he had no time to raid or make war.

Captain Harding was going to demonstrate to the army exactly how his plan would work.

Just as soon as he found the band who had murdered his wife and son and captured his daughter.

Harding went out to talk to Riddle. The roster was complete. The men would be inspected the following morning, and with any luck they would have the supply lists worked out and organized in another day and a half.

"If all goes well, Colt, we should be able to have you on your way in three more days."

They looked at each other.

"Which means somebody could be here from Department Headquarters in San Antonio before we leave," Harding said, slapping his riding crop against the desk top.

"Possible. With almost a nine thousand dollar loss from that Indian raid, some major or light colonel is going to be busting his ass to get out here and make a name for himself."

Harding nodded. "Damnit to hell! See if you can squeeze another twenty-four hours out of that schedule."

"Already have, Colt. It's as tight as I can make it. I'm not sending you off half prepared or half supplied."

They stared at each other again, this time Riddle looked away first. "I've worked out the spread of troops, half from B company and half from A. They'll take their sergeants and officer: that's Lieutenant Oliver and Lieutenant Dan Edwards who used to be in charge of a platoon but was moved up to company commander when Captain Adamson was ordered to San Antonio."

"Edwards, yes, too young for the spot, but we don't have anyone else. It'll have to do. Now try and cut out at least twelve hours for me. I'm going to look at the stock."

On the other side of the fort, across the dusty parade ground in Officer Country, Garland Oliver entered his quarters. After the Gatling gun practice, Oliver had returned the weapon to the special locked cabinet in the weapons room, double locked it and took the keys to the adjutant's office. They were always kept there. He relieved his special detail on the gun and went back to his quarters.

Army standing orders called for the troops in all posts and forts to fall out for drills and "gunnery and horsemanship" practice once each day. It was an order that was almost universally ignored.

Commanders ordered drills and training whenever they thought it might help, often for disciplinary reasons. There was no chance to do even rudimentary target practice. The men in his company had not fired a round in practice during the past six months.

On some posts target practice was considered a waste of good ammunition and too expensive. Some commanders had been charged for the rounds that their men fired during target practice. Lieutenant Oliver had gone around this error in army judgment by giving his men on wood cutting details and on patrols a minimum of ten rounds of practice per patrol. It had helped his men become some of the best shots in the fort.

He was downright embarrassed however by the horsemanship of his men. Most had little or no riding experience when they joined the Cavalry. More than half of the men did well simply to sit their horses during the slow riding on a long march.

A flat out Cavalry charge would find six or eight out of his company actually falling off their mounts. When they got back from this patrol he would fall the men out every afternoon for horsemanship practice.

He took off his saber, dropped his campaign hat on his bunk and washed up in the bowl on the small washstand in his quarters. It was a bachelor's room, ten feet wide as were all the rooms and quarters and shops and stores inside the three-foot thick outer walls. His room had one narrow window looking out onto the parade grounds.

He dropped on his bunk and stared at the spot near the dividing wall and beside his washstand where he had secreted the gold.

Oliver grinned as he remembered how it worked out. Before his troops had left the massacre site of the supply train, he had found time in the darkness and general confusion, to dig up the gold and store it in his saddle bags and in his blanket roll. No one had seen him, he had made sure of that.

The trip back the next morning had been without incident. It had been slow due to the covered wagon carrying the two bodies. Once at the fort he carried his tack and blanket roll into his quarters and quickly stored the gold under the loose floor board where he usually kept a small cache of cash he had built up after being on this post for almost two years.

It had been a simple project to hide the gold, shake out his blankets and have his orderly take his saddlebags back to the tack room. He lay there dreaming how he would spend the money. He hadn't wanted to take the time to count it when he first got back.

There had been no marking on the wooden box. He had thought of putting a blanket over the window late some night, opening the floorboard and making a count. But he decided it was more enjoyable to guess how much was there.

He could resign from the army at any time. His compulsory time was up after West Point. But he should make captain within another year.

He snorted. There had to be five or six thousand dollars in the box. He had not seen the report by the adjutant about the loss. He thought of all the things he could do in San Franciso with six or seven thousand dollars!

He could open his own gambling palace and live like a king the rest of his life. He could have all the women he wanted! He could build a big house and become a respectable merchant! There were a thousand things he could do.

He finished the afternoon's inspection of

the half of his troop that would be going on the patrol. They were in good shape. Now if they could only ride better. Supper in the officers' mess that evening was uninspired, bland and overcooked. He went back to his quarters, rejected Lt. Edwards' offer to play some cards, and settled down behind the small desk he had made from some packing boxes.

He had a list of nearly thirty projects he could do if there were ten thousand dollars in the cache. He worked over the list all evening, then tried to figure out how he could logically resign, without bringing suspicion on himself. He knew that there had been a report made about the missing gold. How long would it be before the Inspector General would send an investigator?

These and a dozen other questions bombarded Oliver as he burned the list of projects over the top of his coal oil lamp chimney, and mashed the ashes in his waste basket.

It wouldn't be long, if he knew the army, before someone began asking questions.

He was in the clear. Nobody could have the slightest inkling that he had anything to do with the missing gold. He went to sleep with a smile on his face, dreaming already about owning his own gambling palace and saloon with six cribs upstairs for the most beautiful whores he could recruit in San Francisco, and all of them would have double-handful sized breasts!

Oliver came awake with a start.

Someone loomed over him.

He felt cold steel, sharp cold steel, pressing against his throat.

"Lieutenant, sir, you make one little sound, and I slit your throat from one ear to the other. That would give you 'bout twenty seconds to live. You want that . . . sir?"

"No! No, of course not," Oliver whispered. He was scratching through his memory for the voice. Then he had it.

Corporal Quentin Pendleton, a sneaky, rank happy little bastard.

"Pendleton, you better have a good reason for doing this, or I'll see you spend twenty years in a Federal prison."

"Got one, Lieutenant. Fact is I got me about eight thousand damn good reasons. I watched you back at the supply wagon train. Saw you open that wooden box, then bury the gold. Then I saw you hide the last of it in your blanket roll just before we went to sleep that night. Strange when we got here how you brought your saddlebags inside before you had them taken with your saddle over to the tack room."

The knife blade pressed harder.

"Hell, I should just do it right now, then find out where you put the gold. You got it here somewhere, all eight thousand dollars worth, right in your quarters. I'd have all night to look. Figure I could find it."

"No! No, don't use the knife. We can work out something, Corporal Pendleton."

"Yeah, like what, high and mighty?"

"Like a thousand dollars!"

The knife moved a fraction of an inch and Oliver felt the blade bite into his flesh and a trickle of blood seep down his neck.

"Dumb, Lieutenant. Shit ass dumb! Thought you officers were smart. Make it fifty/fifty and you got a deal. You make it that way and have it ready for me tomorrow, and I won't turn you in. I won't go to the captain tomorrow morning before breakfast and tell him who stole the gold."

Oliver felt sweat seep down his face and join the trickle of blood down his neck. He had to do this exactly right or he would die. He knew Pendleton, the man was absolutely amoral, who thought only of money. He was a poker player, a gambler, a drinker and he sold his wife for two dollars a throw.

"Yes. Yes, I think we can agree on that. Tomorrow. Now move the blade."

The blade left his throat, but at once the

point touched his chest over his heart. Oliver lay perfectly still.

"This way, big shot officer," Pendleton brayed. "You have the gold in a small carpetbag for me tomorrow. You call me from the barracks and have me deliver it somewhere. I'll stop off at my quarters and dump out the gold and deliver the empty carpetbag. Sound good?"

"Yes, good. I'll make all the arrangements with you tomorrow morning." He swore softly. "Damn, I have wood detail tomorrow. I'll pick a squad of ten men to go cut wood. Why don't you volunteer to come along as the NCO? Then we can work out the rest of the details."

"What details?"

"About where to deliver the bag, what time, all of that."

Pendleton pulled away the knife. He stood up and backed away being careful not to silhouette himself against the window.

"Yeah, okay. I'm easy to get along with. You pay half and I don't remember seeing a damn thing at Buffalo Creek." He laughed softly and a moment later the door opened a crack, then swung wide and a shadow darted out and the door closed.

Lieutenant Oliver lay there a moment, got up and splashed alcohol and bay rum on his nicked throat, then lay down on his bunk and smiled. Tomorrow on the wood gathering detail they would go a little farther out than usual, farther into the edge of the Comanche hunting grounds.

The next morning Oliver had his detail of wood cutters with their wagons ready just after morning mess. They pulled out of the fort and found the small stream to the north and went along it westward. Most of the good sized trees had already been cut for wood near the fort, and now he worked almost five miles west along the creek to a good stand of cottonwoods and some other fair sized trees which Oliver did not have a name for.

Pendleton had volunteered for the detail as the NCO and he put the ten men to work falling, sawing and splitting the wood into usable size and loading it on the wagon. They worked all morning, had a short dinner break, and were nearly done when Oliver and Pendleton walked upstream to the west.

"It's all set then," Oliver said watching Pendleton. "A fifty/fifty split. Four thousand dollars for you. I'll have it in a blue and black carpet bag just before evening mass."

Pendleton frowned slightly. "This is too easy, Lieutenant. I figured you'd be harder to convince."

"What's to argue? You saw me take the

gold, you figure I have it in my quarters. I don't have much bargaining power."

The corporal grinned and bent down and took a long drink from the clear stream. He laughed softly.

"Yeah, I think you're right, Oliver. I've got you over a damn big barrel, and no damn way you can squirm from it, and stay out of prison."

"There is one way, Pendleton," Oliver said.

"What in hell could it be?" Pendleton said looking up as he turned from the water to face his officer.

"This way, you treacherous little bastard!" Oliver said. He held his army issue Smith and Wesson .44 aimed at Pendleton's heart.

"Not a chance in hell you'd shoot me," Pendleton said.

Oliver snorted and shot him twice in the chest, the second round slamming through his heart blasting him into hell a little early. The devil will be pleased.

Oliver fired three more times into the brush. Reloaded and took off his new hat and fired one round through it, then ran back toward the wood cutter.

They had heard the shooting and met him about half way.

"Damned Comanches!" he bellowed at

them. "Stay low, I think I drove them off. One of the hostiles had a rifle. They must have been on a long range hunt."

That afternoon when the wagons came into Fort Comfort with the wood, the first rig held the body of Corporal Quentin Pendleton, and tales of how the whole wood cutting crew had to drive them off. More than eighty rounds had been expended in the brisk engagement with two or more Comanche hunters.

Lieutenant Oliver made a complete report to Lieutenant Riddle, who passed it on to the fort commander. Captain Harding read it with a frown.

"I've never heard of the Comanches sending long range hunting parties out this far. What the hell were they hunting for? The buffalo are all in the other direction."

"Who knows what the Comanches are thinking, Captain? We've got Oliver's statement. I talked to four of the enlisted men on the party and they all agree in principle. Nobody but Oliver saw the hostiles, but that's not unusual. You know how sneaky they can be when they know you're around."

"I know." Captain Harding scowled for a moment. "Hold the report until we get back from the patrol. Has there been any trouble between Oliver and this Pendleton?"

"No record of it. I asked the men the same

thing. Nobody in his company has ever heard of any bad blood there."

Harding thew up his hands. "Hell, sign it and send in the report as a battle casualty. He has a wife on base, right?"

"Yes. I notified her as soon as I found out. She'll probably be returning to the east. They don't have any children."

"Go ahead. I'll countersign it as a killed in action. Now, how are we coming along on this patrol? Can we be ready to leave at noon tomorrow?"

Chapter 6

Little Sadie Harding sat on the lumpy old buffalo robe on the funny looking sled. She couldn't understand why they were moving again. She knew they were Indians, she knew that the thin woman who fed her and held her and put her to sleep was trying to be kind to her. She even understood three or four words the small, thin woman had taught her. But Sadie still wanted her mother. She wanted to go home to the fort, wherever that was.

Cries In The Morning stood watching her small daughter. Laughing Golden Hair's blue eyes were filled with wonder and worry.

"I know you don't understand any of this, Small Wonder," Cries In The Morning said gently. "But soon you will, we will learn more words. We move a lot, it is the way of the People. We have a large herd of horses and mules and they must have forage. If we stay too long in one place, they eat off all the hair of Mother Earth and it dies."

Cries In The Morning finished folding the heavy buffalo hides that had been carefully stitched together with strong buffalo sinew to form the tipi cover. She had a huge task every time they moved to take down the tipi, fold the cover, lash the tall poles onto the travois, and pack everything she and her husband Running Wolf owned. Most of it went in buffalo robes tied to the travois. Sometimes in the summer there were rawhide boxes they could use.

She had done it so many times that Cries In The Morning had packing down to a routine. She had to decide whether to tie Laughing Golden Hair on a pony, or to let her sit on the travois.

The tipis came down now all over the camp, as the Eagle Band prepared to move.

Walking White Eagle had heard how the Pony Soldiers had penetrated through the marsh and into the secret valley itself. He had sent two scouts to watch for the soldiers, and when they came back with the news of the discovery of the valley, the whole camp had been in an uproar.

But more scouts soon came reporting the Pony Soldiers did not push forward. There were only four handfuls of them and they held back, cared for an injured man, and then retraced their steps.

White Eagle sent scouts to track the Pony Soldiers until he was sure they were heading back to the army fort. He had worried about how clever the Pony Soldiers had been, how they had avoided the false trails and even figured out the marsh. This was no ordinary Pony Soldier who hunted them.

White Eagle decided that they would move on in a week. It was nearing time for the first hunt, when they would take as much meat as they could. It would be the first of three hunts to provide them with the needed food for the long winter to come. They would move well to the north and west even toward the Staked Plains, but they would not go that far.

White Eagle looked around at the camp that had stretched along the stream for more than three long arrow shots. There were now over fifty tipis in his band. It seemed to keep growing with each passing day.

Some families came from War Kettle's band, unhappy with the way he was turning from the old ways. War Kettle had been to talk with the round-eyes twice, and both times came back with many gifts – but also with word that the whites wanted only peace with the Comanche. White Eagle knew the whites wanted peace – if the Comanche would do exactly as the white generals wanted them to!

White Eagle sat on his new war pony, Flying Wind. He had learned his lessons well, and in the upcoming hunt he would be able to prove his worth. If he could chase the thundering buffalo and race flank to flank with the huge marvelous beasts, then he would be a true hunting pony as well as a war pony.

Flying Wind would have his chance soon. They were headed for a new summer camp, farther north and west than ever before, but it seemed the only alternative to harassment by the Pony Soldiers. They seemed to be everywhere this summer.

The head of the Eagle band saw with satisfaction that the camp was packing up quickly. Sometimes they had to make fast moves, in case of a sudden attack by enemy tribes or even by the Pony Soldiers.

His wives had his large tipi down quickly and everything packed. Now they waited, each on her horse beside the two travois. They set a good example.

Packing was woman's work. All the warriors were mounted with bow and arrows, lance and shield, ready to defend the camp from any attack. Fighting was man's work, he must be ready at any moment all day and night to fight for the band.

A dozen young boys, eight to twelve summers, charged past him on their ponies, shouting and laughing. Moving was one of the best times for them. They got to herd the horses and mules, to race up and down the line of march. They were future warriors and now was the time they began to perfect their horsemanship, and to use their bows. Each boy had a bow made especially for him, according to his height.

The boys raced off, slashing through the dismantling camp, upsetting some yet unpacked racks for drying meat, scattering possessions and raising the angry glances of the women working hard at packing.

White Eagle signalled Always Smiling, and she moved forward, leading the pack horse hauling the first travois. They would lead the line of march as usual, as was befitting the leader's first wife. She would also be in place if anyone needed her and her deep and all encompassing medicine bag.

She had learned about the healing roots and berries and shrubs and herbs from her mother, who had been medicine woman for many, many winters with the Comanche. There had been so much to understand, but slowly Always Smiling became as good at working with roots and powders and barks and potions from the bag as her mother.

White Eagle left two scouts in the hidden valley just above the one the Pony Soldiers had found. They were to stay there for four days, then follow the band north and west, remaining four days behind the band as security. After a week they would come into the new camp.

White Eagle sat at the departing point from the second hidden valley. They would go over a small rise and into a plain so flat on many days the best eyes in the band could not see the other side. He had divided his band into six groups, and sent them off at angles to their line of travel.

He took the most direct route, but made loops and circles to confuse anyone following them. In his heart he knew that no amount of trail trickery could disguise such a large group. They had sixty travois, and more than a thousand horses, ponies and mules. The herd made a river across the virgin grasslands if kept together.

The small white girl riding a travois near the head of the column stared in wonder at the mass of people and horses. At first she had whimpered in fear, but Cries In The Morning came back and walked her pretty spotted pony beside the litter and said one word over and over.

"Toquet, toquet . . . toquet."

It was one of the few words of the People that Sadie Harding understood. It meant, "it is well," and when she heard the word, she could smile and nod. Cries In the Morning went back to the front of the travois and Talks A Lot came beside Sadie.

The young Indian girl talked and talked, but never once did she say *toquet*, and Sadie, known to the Indians now as Laughing Golden Hair, did not understand a word she said.

The rolling, rocking motion of the buffalo robe stretched between the poles, affected Sadie, and soon she nodded, then went to sleep.

Talks A Lot smiled, slipped off her pony and worked the small white body deeply into the robes and packed supplies so she would not tumble out. Soon Talks A Lot would have a baby of her own, a son for the chief, a future chief of the Comanche! Talks A Lot vaulted back on her pony's back and watched over the small *yo-oh-hobt pa-pi*, the yellow hair. A small smile wreathed her face as she thought of the child and held one hand on her swelling belly.

Seven days they worked across the broad plain. Some days they traveled twenty miles, some only eight or ten. Each night they picked a campsite near water and good forage for the animals, but they did not pause to put up the tipis.

That evening the leaders of the band sat around a small council fire and talked. Each man gave his ideas about the hunt to come. Advance scouts had reported back that there were two large herds of buffalo grazing just over a small rise. The band was down wind of them so no Indian scent would carry that way.

White Eagle listened to the comments, then stood.

"What you say is important and we will do as we always have done. With the morning we will be working quickly into the herd and taking as many of Mother Earth's buffalo as possible. We will use bow and arrows with the large hunting points of steel, and we will use our lances. No rifles are to be fired. They will frighten the buffalo before we have killed enough to make a good hunting camp."

Some of the warriors grumbled but there was no real opposition. Since the wagon wheel raid, White Eagle had given out half of the rifles, and instructed each warrior carefully how to use the weapon. But they agreed on the noise. There would be at least one more traditional buffalo hunt.

All that evening and into the night the warriors readied their lances, sharpened arrow points, finished a spare bow just in case one was lost or broken. Fires burned late that night as the old men of the band told of their amazing exploits in hunting the hulking buffalo in days gone by.

Wears His Coat had the best tale, and several of the warriors paused around a fire to listen.

"We were well below the Colorado and surprised a herd of not more than a hundred head that had wandered off from the rest. They were moving back north when we hit them.

"Twenty-seven braves rode out of the grass and charged them. I had only four arrows that day, tipped with black flint and sharp.

"We stormed at them from three sides. The cows gave the alarm and they bellowed and stampeded directly at us. You don't turn a buffalo stampede. Instead we waited for them, got to the side and began shooting buffalo.

"In those days every bull was over two thousand pounds. Huge shaggy brutes that stood six feet high at the shoulder. When an old buff decides to go one way, nothing changes his mind. He keeps right on running through and over trees and rivers and sometimes cliffs.

"I rode up beside this one and he glared at me from his big eye and I shot my first arrow. It went in just behind his right shoulder, down and through his heart. He dropped like a rock in a still pond, and I went after another one."

The stories by the old men would continue until late in the night. They didn't have to get up early to go on the hunt.

No camp was set up here, they would rest and move on in the morning. The warriors would go on the hunt and the women and children and the horse herders would move up only when there was word that there had been buffalo killed and the hunting camp would then be moved close to the kill and everyone set to work.

Cries In The Morning held Laughing Golden Hair a moment more, then put her down on a thick buffalo robe and went back to the small cooking fire. She returned a moment later with two pointed sticks, each with a piece of roasted meat on it. She held one out to the small white girl who took it eagerly and bit through the slightly burned exterior to the delicious pink meat inside.

She decided it was rabbit or maybe deer meat. It didn't matter, she was hungry and the meat was roasted and done. She let the dripping grease fall on the ground. Sadie decided that she liked the outside camping best. The tipi was all right, but it usually smelled so strange.

For a minute she wondered if her father would ever come and take her home. It had been a long time since her mother had left. And where was Yale, her big brother?

Tears welled up in her soft blue eyes, and when Cries In The Morning saw them she tenderly brushed them away.

"*Hi, tai toquet,* hello friend, it's all right," Cries In The Morning said, and gave Sadie the rest of the roast meat she was eating. Sadie took it, and stared at the strange smile on the dark, lined face.

"Thank you," Sadie said, and Cries In The Morning bobbed her head and went back to the fire to roast more of the venison.

When daylight came, thirty-five warriors and young boys, almost warriors, held their ponies in check at the edge of a small fringe of trees. Just beyond lay a natural grazing land and there the herd of less than a hundred buffalo had made its bed-ground. The cows and calves lay in the center, the bulls on the outer rim.

White Eagle and the other hunters were checking themselves and their equipment. He had chosen to ride bareback, so Flying Wind would have that much less weight to carry. He had reins twenty feet long that would trail his mount. Then if he got knocked off by the buffalo, he would have a chance to grab the trailing reins so Flying Wind would pull him free of the murderous bison hooves.

White Eagle wore only moccasins, his breechclout and his skinning knife on his belt. Now he took a coiled bowstring of sinew from between his legs where he had kept it warm and dry from the morning dampness.

Quickly he strung his bow. If the sinew was too dry it would break when he pulled the bow. When it became damp it stretched. Now it was just right.

He balanced his bow on his thighs and shifted the quiver so it extended over his left shoulder where he could reach for an arrow easily with his right hand. Eight arrows rested there, each with his special mark on them, a bright, wide band of red near the feathers.

It was his arrow "name." Anyone finding

an arrow so marked would return it to its owner. Arrows, good ones used for hunting and war, were hard to make and valued highly.

The buffalo were wary. The big animals did not have exceptionally good eyesight, but their sense of smell was highly developed.

White Eagle chose five arrows and held them in his hand as he gripped his bow. He would ride without the use of his hands.

A moment later the wind shifted, drifting the human scent to the animals. A cow snorted noisily. A bull bellowed, then three cows got to their feet and gave some kind of a signal. In moments the herd would be stampeding across the open plains.

White Eagle gave the cry of the eagle and the warriors and riders charged forward. The herd had lifted to its feet and led by a huge bull well over six feet at the shoulders, pounded away from the pony riders.

No buffalo can outrun a Comanche hunting pony, and quickly the hunters closed on the trailing members of the herd. The calves were passed up, and two younger boys worked together on a big cow that weighed over a thousand pounds. They took turns shooting arrows into her from their galloping ponies. The third arrow found its mark and the cow bison stumbled, tripped and tumbled over and over on the grassy plains.

The boys whooped in delight and rushed after another target.

White Eagle urged Flying Wind faster as he closed in on the leader of the stampede, the huge buffalo with the heavy shoulder coat and bare rear quarters where his winter coat had been rubbed free.

White Eagle had an arrow notched and came up on the right side of the beast. He nudged Flying Wind closer to the big, charging animal until the horse was barely a bow length away. White Eagle aimed and fired the arrow in one smooth movement, hardly conscious of aiming, knowing where the arrow had to go and willing it to its target. The arrow drove into the soft area behind the heaving shoulder, passed through part of a lung and daggered through the bison's heart before the arrow tip emerged out the far side of the dying creature.

The big animal continued for ten more charging steps before his front legs collapsed and he went down in a long skid that broke both his front legs as he drove his twenty-four hundred pounds of weight against them.

White Eagle pulled to one side and viewed the hunt. He saw more than a dozen animals down, and warriors still in pursuit. He urged Flying Wind forward again, picked out a bull and nudged his hunting pony faster so they pulled up beside the heaving, snorting animal. The big bull never looked their way. He was the king of the prairie and nothing was going to stop him from running straight ahead if he chose to. His small brain had picked his direction and nothing would dissuade him.

The Comanche warrior changed his mind with another broad tipped arrow and cut through thick buffalo hair and hide and found a vital region sending the big animal into a stumbling, snorting demise.

White Eagle pulled up. He was half a mile away from the first kill. Far enough. He turned and counted the dead animals as he trotted back to the first one. They had dispatched twenty-eight buffalo! It would be half enough to fill their winter rawhide boxes with pemmican and racks of dried jerky.

He sat on Flying Wind and patted his neck as the leader of the band saw his wives running forward with their knives. Soon the butchering would start, and the choicest bits of delicacies would be eaten raw.

Always Smiling sank to her knees beside the first bull that had barely stopped its death struggle and slit open his belly and thrust her arm into the body cavity hunting the liver. She found it and cut it free and held it up to the first warrior who came by.

The raw livers were reserved for the hunters.

She continued exploring the animal. She found yellow tallow from the bull's loins, and popped the soft mass into her mouth. For a moment she moaned in delight. Prairie Flower came up quickly and cut out some of the entrails and chewed on them with a look of total rapture on her thin face. It had been nearly a year since she had tasted anything so delicious.

Something Good cut out the big bull's heart and set it aside since it would be honored to encourage the buffalo to prosper and multiply.

When the delicacies were eaten, everyone pitched in to do the work of butchering the twenty-eight animals. They were skinned carefully, the robes would keep them warm this winter.

Quickly drying racks were set up. These racks were often five feet high and that wide, with hooks in rows to hold the strips of buffalo meat to be dried into jerky so it didn't spoil.

Everyone worked quickly. Usually it took five women and girls to cut up one animal and get the meat hung on drying racks. They all knew that any of the meat not set to drying before noon would be spoiled by the next day. Even the hunters and warriors stepped in and worked over the animals. This was their winter's food supply and butchering work was acceptable.

Usually the hunter's family butchered out the animal he had killed. It was a hard job. First the animal was turned on its side, then the belly split open and the heavy hide skinned up to the backbone on one side.

Next the meat was cut out and strips made for drying. When one side was done, ponies were used to turn the buffalo over to do the same thing on the other side.

The hunting camp had been set up among the fringe of trees near the small stream. Packhorses were used to haul the strips of meat back to the hunting camp where they were hung on the drying racks.

Almost every part of the buffalo was used by the Comanches. They got the sinews from along the spine, they scooped out the brains and saved them in a stomach liner. They would be used later in the tanning process.

Bladders would become medicine pouches, the bones would be made into shovels, splints, saddle trees, awls, scrapers and even ornaments. The bull's scrotum was cut off and became a rattle for some of the dances. Paunch liners from the buffalo's stomach became water bottles. Even the hooves and feet would be used for glue and rattles. The small, curved buffalo horns would become fireproof coal containers for fire starting on long trips, and for holding black powder.

Hair from the hides that were tanned would become stuffing in saddle pads and shields and pillows. Some of it would be braided and made into ropes and halters and surcingles and headdresses.

It was too early in the summer for prime hides. There would be more hunts later in the fall and even into December to get absolutely prime hides when the fur was thickest.

When the last piece of meat was hung on the racks, and the last brisket taken and wrapped in hide, and the last bit of the buffalo saved and measured for use, the weary band returned to the hunting camp.

They splashed themselves in the stream to wash away the blood of the butchering. There would be a dance that night, a celebration of the good hunt, and the hunters would tell of their skill in taking down a two thousand pound beast with a single arrow.

Cries In The Morning had left Laughing Golden Hair in the hunting camp with friends as she went to the butchering. Now she reclaimed the small one and saw that she had fallen asleep. Cries In The Morning picked her up and rocked her on the way to her small and low lean-to, which they always made at hunting camp. It was quicker than putting up the tipis each time. Also it was summer and warm.

Cries In The Morning lay the golden child with the blue eyes down on her small raised bedstead among the softest robes she owned, and watched her for a moment. Truly she was a fortunate woman. She not only had a child, she had a wonder child, with golden hair and eyes the color of the morning sky. She smiled softly and brushed some of the yellow hair from the small girl's eyes.

Chapter 7

Lieutenant John Riddle, adjutant of Fort Comfort and second in command stood beside Captain Colt Harding's desk. He had a strained, worried look and Harding shook his head.

"Not a chance you can talk me out of it, John. I'm going. I'm going to find those bastards and cut their balls off and stuff them down their throats, then I'm going to make them suffer the same way my Milly did. You can bank on it!"

"Orders," Riddle said slowly. "What orders are we operating under, in case somebody asks me?"

"Standing orders, John, the way I told you before. The commander of every fort or installation has wide latitude in the pursuit and punishment of hostiles who attack, kill, kidnap, either military or civilian personnel, or who destroy valuable government or civilian property. I'd say the Comanches did both, and I'm going after them."

Riddle stepped aside. He waved the captain to the door.

"Your patrol will be ready in an hour. You have enough salt pork, bacon, beans and hardtack for six weeks. That's as much as we can scrape up until the next supply train gets through. You told me to use my judgment on the supplies."

"I said two months, damnit!"

"The fort garrison will be on half rations for the last two weeks you're out as it is. Seemed fair to me. If you order me to, I'll increase the supplies on your wagon, and cut the fort troopers to half rations starting now."

Captain Harding kicked his desk with a well worn boot and swore under his breath.

"You know I won't ask you to do that. We'll be back in six weeks – or we'll live off the land, what there is to live off."

He marched to the door, opened it and without a glance behind him strode through the outer office to the small porch.

Corporal Swenson had his black waiting for him. Colt stepped into the saddle and saw Oliver bring the line of troopers to attention.

He rode to the center in front of the Cavalrymen lined up four deep and stood in his stirrups.

"Men! You know what we've lost ... fifteen good men and three civilians. We're going to pay back the Comanches in blood. It won't be easy and it won't be quick. Let's ride."

It was straight up noon.

Oliver ordered the men into a column of fours and they led out behind the commander. A lead Tonkawa scout rode just behind the captain. Oliver sent two Tonkawas ahead a half mile indicating a direction and a landmark. They would ride directly to the hidden valley.

The special patrol was set up as usual for an army unit. Each trooper carried his carbine or rifle, one hundred and fifty rounds of ammunition, half a pup tent, three days rations of salt pork, hardtack, dry beans and coffee. He had one blanket, a rubber sheet as a ground cloth, one extra uniform and five pair of socks and low cut shoes. The Pony Soldiers had one other item that was indispensable, fifteen pounds of grain for their mounts.

With scouts out ahead, two man security details on each side and a four man rear guard, the unit moved out. Directly behind the column of fours came the Gatling gun and its caisson, then the supply wagon, and one empty wagon that would be used as an ambulance if needed.

The column moved forward smartly for the first four miles, then they had a small stream to cross. It took an hour to get the two wagons through the stream. It was finally accomplished with six added horses with ropes pulling the heavy wagon through the soft bottom.

The Tonkawa scouts would not help push the wagons out of the stream. They said that Mother Earth did not like the wagons or she would not make them stuck. They should leave them where they were so not to make Mother Earth angry.

They made only eight miles before it was time to stop. Most days they had to start camp two hours before dark. The troops had chores to do.

Their horses came first. They set up picket lines for the horses and mules, then fed and watered each one.

Guards were set up on the camp perimeter, and a wood detail was ordered out to bring back enough wood for the cooking fires. In this location there was almost no wood available, so the detail gathered up gunny sacks full of buffalo chips and turned them over to the sergeant in charge.

This night the two men pup tents were set up in a straight line by squads. The men pounded in the stakes and sergeants lined them up. With that out of the way permission was given to start the evening meal.

On a long march the only hot meal of the day was at night. Since no cooks came along, each man had to do his own cooking. As was the case with most soldiers, they had discarded the official mess kit, a tin plate and a collapsible skillet, and instead carried a small solid skillet and a big tin cup from the sutter's supply.

Sergeant Casemore was an old hand at range cooking. He dug out a portion of salt pork and parboiled it in the skillet, then threw out the water and fried it in the skillet until it crackled.

Earlier he had roasted the raw coffee beans in the skillet and ground the cooked beans into powder with the help of a pair of rocks and his knife. Then he boiled his coffee in the big cup sitting on rocks at the edge of the small cooking fire.

Captain Harding had the luxury of a Sibley conical tent, with a folding cot from the supply wagon to sleep on. His orderly and the bugler slept just outside in their two man tent. Usually Corporal Swenson cooked for all the officers on the trip. Supplies were drawn from the supply wagon, but the food was the same as the men ate.

Sometimes they had dried fruits, raisins and condensed milk, but this trip there were no extras, and the officers had to settle for the same salt pork, hardtack and beans the men were issued.

After the meal the men were free to spend what leisure time they might have as they chose. There were always card games that went until dark, some singing, letter writing and talk. The usual chatter about the officers and complaints about the army were in full swing on this night when Sergeant Casemore made the rounds of his men.

Each company had kept its officers and sergeants together, so they could function as units. One of the privates saw his sergeant and called to him.

"Sarge, it true that we're going to keep riding until we track down that band of Comanches, no matter if it takes all summer?"

Casemore snorted. "Who the hell told you that, son? We're on a search patrol, try to find the hostiles if we can. If we can't we come back and try again. Captain Harding ain't crazy. He knows about how far we can go and still get back to the fort without eating our mules."

He paused and looked at the soldier, who wasn't much more than a year past eighteen.

"You ever et mule meat, boy? It's not much good. But it'll keep you alive. I'm proof of that. Two years ago coming back from a two month patrol we ran out of rations and killed a mule every third day and threw away what the critter was packing. Ate up eight mules that way but we got back to the fort without losing a man."

Casemore told the men they better be thinking about bedding down. First call would be coming early.

It did.

Life on the trail for the men began at 4:45 A.M. when the troopers rolled out of their blankets and dressed if they had taken off more than their boots.

Ten minutes later reveille and stable call sounded. They had five minutes to saddle their horses and harness the mules.

At five A.M. sharp mess call bugled across

the Texas plains. Now they had a half hour to fix and eat their morning meal, which usually was coffee and hardtack, and some dried fruit if they had any.

General call came at 5:30, when they struck the camp. It was the busiest, hectic time when they tore down the tents, packed their gear on their mounts and stored any equipment in the wagons.

At 5:45 it was Boots and Saddles, when the Cavalrymen mounted their horses.

Ten minutes later came Fall In, and the entire group assembled in marching order in a column of fours.

Promptly at six A.M., Captain Harding lifted his saber and swung it forward. Lieutenants shouted the marching order. Sergeants down the column repeated the orders, and the long line of blue shirted troopers moved out across the prairie of western Texas.

The Tonkawa scouts not in the lead, rode to one side, out of the line of march, but close by, continually amazed at the routines of the roundeyes, but happy to have their own ration of hardtack and salt pork.

Now, as often happened, Captain Harding gave the order that six of the Tonkawas should swing away from the line of march on a hunting expedition. They should bring back any game they could by use of their bows and arrows or carbines. Most of the Indians had learned to use the rifles well and often could shoot better than most of the poorly trained Cavalrymen.

Casemore gave the orders that were passed down to him. He picked out six of the Tonkawa scouts and told them what to do. They grinned and laughed. They were getting army pay for hunting! It seemed like child's play to them, and they eagerly surged away from the main party, indicating they would be back to the line by midday.

Captain Harding rode at the head of the company sized patrol. He had enough rounds for each man for a major campaign. He had brought a box of a hundred sticks of the new dynamite, and had figured out a special use for it.

Grenades and grenadiers had long been military terms, but the U.S. Cavalry had no small hand held bomb for its troops. He had devised such a weapon that was devastating, easy to produce and carry and while not totally reliable, could be counted on in six out of seven times.

He had experimented with the new stick dynamite until he had precisely what he wanted. He had cut the twelve inch stick of explosive in half and wired the halves together. Then he used sticky tape and large headed roofing nails, and taped the nails around the six inch sticks of explosive.

By careful planning he could bind fifty of the roofing nails to the dynamite bomb.

By inserting a six inch fuse with a blasting cap pushed into the powder, he had an easy to carry, easy to use and deadly hand bomb. When it detonated it sent long roofing nails blasting out in all directions like shrapnel. He hoped to be able to use the new bombs against the Comanches.

Before he left the fort, Captain Harding had a detail of men fashion fifty of the small hand bombs. The six inch fuse usually burned in thirty seconds. Fuse was rated to burn a foot a minute, but as with any new weapon there were problems. Some burned much faster, some slower.

He had experimented and soon cut the fuse length to three inches, so the bomb would explode in fifteen seconds. He was sure he would find ample use for the hand bombs.

The route was familiar and fairly level across the flatness of western Texas. They crossed the upper reaches of the Colorado of Texas and pushed on toward the middle fork of the Brazos.

The second day the hunters came back with a good sized deer, which they had dressed out, and quartered. Every man had at least a small portion of fresh meat that night to cook. The Indians had eaten the heart and liver and most of the entrails raw as was their custom.

The fifth day they forded the central fork of the Brazos and worked toward the marsh and the hidden valley. Two miles from it, Captain Harding called a halt at a small bluff near water and forage. The troop camped with its back to the bluff for protection and rested.

Harding took reports from his scouts. They had found no hostiles in the first valley across the marsh. He ordered them to scout the next valley and come back with a report before dark.

Again the Tonkawas reported no sign of the hated Comanches. They had camped in the second valley for two or three weeks, the Tonkawas said, but had left in orderly fashion, evidently in small groups at a time and in various directions. There was no way to be sure which direction the main band was headed.

Harding went into his Sibley, sat on his folding canvas chair and looked at the pictures of his wife. He had no picture at all of Yale or of Sadie.

He slammed his fist into his open palm.

Damnit to hell! What an ordeal she was going through! Living with those savages, those butcherers.

He paced his tent, then went outside and walked a half mile up a small creek and threw rocks in the water. When he came back he had his plan. It was generally against army policy to send out Indian scouts alone, but in this case it was all he could do. He sent for the head Indian scout, called Big Ear.

The Tonkawa was about twenty-five years old, had a saber slash on one cheek and insisted on wearing an army officer shirt with corporal stripes on it. Nobody minded but the corporals, but they were not ready to challenge him in a knife fight.

Big Ear had picked up English quickly and now communicated effectively with some English words and signs.

"Take all of your scouts," Captain Harding told him. "You'll get three days' rations. Ride down those trails. Do at least sixty miles a day. Many, many miles. Find out where the Comanches are heading."

At last Big Ear understood. He laughed softly. With three days' army rations he could lead his raiding party on a two week spree! They could find some cabins and have a feast! But quickly he changed his mind. There were no settlers this far out, and the Pony Soldiers would shoot him if he did not obey his orders.

But it would be good to find the Comanche! He could smell the soup cooking now! Quickly he hurried to the place assigned to the Indians for the camp, and spoke to the warriors. They would leave as soon as they drew their rations. Each scout had a carbine and a hundred and sixty rounds of ammunition.

For three days Big Ear and his Tonkawas rode hard. They tracked the puny efforts of the Comanches to hide their trails. The members of the band came together and separated, crossed trails, back tracked and split up again and again, but always they rejoined and always they moved northwest.

They soon left the land of the Brazos and ventured deeper into West Texas, well out of their usual hunting and camping grounds. The fourth day Big Ear could see the looming presence of the cap rock escarpment to the west. They had penetrated all the way to the flat Texas plateau just below the Staked Plains!

The main party of the Comanche band had assembled now and with no more trickery angled directly for the Staked Plains. They hit a small river that seemed to run straight into the cap rock. An hour later Big Ear saw where the Comanche band vanished. They had either vaporized and blew away, or ridden in the creek where it sliced into a narrow gorge that knifed into the eight hundred foot high cliffs where the Staked Plains reared up out of the Texas landscape.

Big Ear and his scouts stared at the contradiction, then turned and rode back toward the Pony Soldiers' camp. For some reason the Comanches had retreated all the way to the Staked Plains. Big Ear was not sure how they climbed to the top of the barricade, but the stream must be the pathway.

His men were disappointed that they would not feast on Comanche soup, but he promised them that soon their hunger would be satisfied.

The Tonkawas had been gone seven days when they rode into the small camp near the bluff. Captain Harding had about decided they had deserted. He told his officers that he would give the savages twenty-four hours to return, then he would declare them deserters, and leave for the fort.

Big Ear rode in with two hours to spare. He and Private Escobar who understood some of the Indian lingo, sat down outside the captain's tent and talked for two hours with the captain, before the Fort Commander understood fully what his scouts had found.

"The Staked Plains? They must be two hundred miles from here. Why the hell did the hostiles go way up there?"

Big Ear heard the question, and understood it, but he had no answer for the Pony Soldier captain. He felt as if they should smoke a pipe, but there was none. He indicated that was the end of his report. The captain waved him away and began pacing up and down in front of his Sibley tent.

'What the hell are those hostiles running that far for?" Colt Harding asked the harsh Texas plains. The soft chattering of the creek, and the whispers of the wind would not give him an answer.

The following morning at 4:45 first call sounded from the bugler's lips and the troops swung into action. Promptly at 6:00 A.M. the men rode out, heading back for the fort. They made better time on the way back, and in four hard days rode near Fort Comfort just before sundown.

Lieutenant Riddle rode out to meet the patrol as soon as his lookouts reported the dust trail.

"That's about the size of it, Captain. His name is Major Zachery, he's from the Inspector General's staff in San Antonio Department of Texas headquarters. He's been interviewing the men involved in the gold problem. The rest of the loss he says is clearly the action of the Comanche.

"His one theme is that there is a one hundred percent chance that one of the men in our command stole the gold. Indians do not understand gold. It's too soft to make arrowheads or scrapers. He's got the whole fort on edge and the men are bitching and fighting among themselves."

"And he can't wait to get at the rest of the men who were on the rescue detail?" Colt asked.

"Right. He's panting. Especially wants to talk to you and to Lieutenant Oliver."

"Figures."

The two officers and friends, rode in silence for a quarter of a mile.

"Damnit, Colt, the major is probably right. Half a dozen of the men in that detail had a chance to find and steal that gold. Eight thousand dollars is as much cash money as an enlisted man would make in thirty-two years!"

Colt adjusted the two six-guns at his sides and stared hard ahead. "It's a temptation worth a man's time, I'll admit that. But most of these men don't have the ambition or the good sense to try to steal that gold. If we find out who the man is, I can guarantee you it will be a surprise to everyone."

Harding turned, ordered Oliver to bring in the patrol and he and Riddle galloped the last quarter mile into the Fort.

A half hour later, Harding had taken a sponge bath in a bucket of hot water Swenson brought him, had put on a clean uniform and combed out his beard and pasted down his hair.

He asked Swenson to bring the major in.

Major Alexander Zachery was barely five feet five inches tall. He was the shortest major Harding had ever seen. The small man wore a Van Dyke beard that came to a sharp point, and the rest trimmed precisely. Over his left eye he fixed a monocle that draped from a gold chain that circled his neck.

He stared at Harding for a moment, then let the glass fall from his eye on its chain and returned the captain's salute. Zachery stepped forward and held out his hand.

"Nasty business, Captain, I heard about your loss. My condolences. Did you track down the bastards?"

"No sir, I'm afraid not."

"Pity. We'll find them. Do you know which band it was?"

"No sir. My Tonkawa scouts say it could be one of three different bands in this area. We're working on it."

"Good, good." They both sat down and the major hesitated.

"Major Zachery, I understand you've been conducting an investigation on my post into the missing government property."

"That's right. I have no doubt at all that one or more of your men on that escort greeting party stole the gold, all eight thousand dollars worth."

"You have all the names from those rosters?"

"Yes, the first party, and the men who went back to bring in the wagons. Many of them were with you on your patrol."

"Give the men a day, could you, Major? It was a frustrating and a hard ride."

"I can do that. You had no casualties?"

"No sir. The guilty party must still be in the fort . . . except for messengers. We send out one a week with dispatches heading for Austin."

"I checked. None of the messengers sent so far were involved."

"Good. Now, Major, could I share a drink with you. I need one after that patrol."

"Help yourself, Captain, I don't drink." The major stood, nodded to Harding who had taken a bottle of good whiskey from his desk drawer.

"See you at supper," the major said, his eyes showing his disapproval as he walked to the door.

Chapter 8

Major Alexander Zachery sat at the first table at the far end of the enlisted men's mess hall. He listened to what the private in front of him said. The major had told the trooper to stand at ease, which the man did, his hands clasped tightly behind his back, his feet eighteen inches apart, his eyes straight ahead.

Kirk MacTavish, private from New York City, was so scared he could hardly breathe. He'd never even *seen a major before*, let alone been talked to by one. He'd always been frightened of officers, they were not like ordinary men. Now he stammered and sweated, and tried to remember.

"Near as I can recall, sir, I never seen no one go near the wagons after we found them. Our lead party of three got there first, made sure nobody was alive and then Corporal Ingles pulled us off fifty yards, told us to stay put. He hightailed it back to the main party."

"And you never approached the wagons yourself?"

"No sir. I ain't that fond of looking at

scalped bodies, especially since I knew some of the troopers."

"Did you see the man with you approach the wagons during the time before Corporal Ingles left and the arrival of your captain and Lieutenant Oliver?"

"No sir. He never moved either. We even stayed mounted, case the hostiles came back."

"Fine, now try and relax, MacTavish. You're not on trial here. This is an inquiry, all unofficial. You were in the area for the next six or seven hours, then?"

"No sir, longer. We stayed until morning before we started back with the wagon and the two dead . . . civilians."

"So the part of A company not on the pursuit detail stayed near the wagons overnight, some seventy-five men?"

"Yes sir. It was near dark before we got the troopers buried and our tents set up. It wasn't a good company street, sir, nobody inspected, they weren't lined up right . . ."

"Yes, Private MacTavish, I can imagine. Death has a way of upsetting a routine." The major frowned. This was going to take a lot longer than he figured. He might have to interview all ninety-five men from Company A. One or more of those twenty men who went on the chase could have found the gold before the midnight departure time.

"How much money do you make a month, Private?"

"Twelve dollars, sir. But there's laundry and the tab at the sutler, and . . . usually not much left."

"So eight thousand dollars to you is a fortune?"

"Land sakes yes, sir. More money than I ever hope to see or to own, even to dream about."

"Thank you, Private MacTavish. That will be all."

MacTavish snapped a salute that was far from perfect. The major returned it with a perfunctory wave and Kirk walked quickly from the nearby doorway. As he went out, the next man in line entered, his campaign hat under his arm.

Across the wide parade grounds in his office, Captain Harding listened to his adjutant.

"Second day of the major's inquiry. So far he's talked to forty-three men. He's hearing about the same thing from most of them. He wants to talk to everyone on the trip from A company, regardless of whether they went on the volunteer chase group with you, or came back the next morning, stayed as guards, or went back with mules to drive in the wagons."

"The man has an all summer's job. I'm more interested in the Comanche. Why in hell did they run off to the Staked Plains?"

"Maybe they always do this time of year," Riddle suggested.

"The Tonkawas say usually the Comanches never get that far west, at least not lately."

"Maybe some ritual, some ceremony. You know how tied to nature most of the Indian religious rites are."

"You don't think they were simply running away from my patrol?"

"No. They probably didn't even know you came any farther than the first valley. They would have scouts out watching for you. They knew the minute you turned back."

"The first time."

"That was enough. By now they have a cold trail."

Harding stood and paced across his office. "So you're saying I should just quit? That the trail is so cold I'll never find Sadie?"

Riddle shook his head. "Not at all. But it looks like there isn't going to be a chance to get Sadie back right away. There are sources. The white hunters out there, still a few trappers around who know the Indians, the traders, the comancheros and a few friendly Indians. We put out the word that there is a small blonde blue-eyed girl out there with the Comanches we want back.

"We watch and wait and try to get some information to tie down which band has little Sadie."

"That could be six months or a year from now before we got any information! What will happen to Sadie?"

"Colt, we need a starting point. We can't charge all over Texas and Indian territories looking for Sadie without knowing something about where she is."

"Damnit, John, I have to do something!" Colt bellowed. They glared at each other for a moment without rancor. Each man trying to find a solution to the problem. If they didn't it would tear Colt Harding apart, get him cashiered out of the service and sent on a lonely trek searching for his lost daughter in a harsh and unforgiving land filled with his mortal enemies.

Slowly Colt began to nod. He stared out the small window into the large courtyard parade ground.

"I have an idea. Help me work it out. Every army campaign ever waged was successful or better because of good intelligence, scouting reports, information. Right now that's what I need for my campaign. I need to know which band, and where that band of Comanches is. Right, John?"

"Absolutely, but how..."

"So I get the intelligence."

"We can't keep sending out company sized patrols. Division is going to start asking questions, looking for some Indian kill figures or reports of raids..."

"Right! John! Exactly right. So we don't send out company sized thrusts. We do it smaller."

"Smaller could mean a whole platoon getting wiped out," John Riddle said.

"Yes, again you're right. How can I do this so I don't get in trouble with Division, and so I protect my men, and still get the job done?"

Captain Harding stared at the big map of western Texas for a long time without saying a word. Then he turned and went to his door. In the outer office he pointed at Corporal Swenson.

"My horse, Corporal. Saddled, canteen and a pair of binoculars. Let me know when you're ready."

John leaned against the door frame.

"You're going out by yourself, alone?"

"I've been called stupid, but I'm not that dumb. I'm going to do some high level planning, and I can do that best in the saddle. With a saddle thumping me on the butt I seem to think better, somehow. Alone, I'll be back before the noon mess call."

A half hour later, Colt Harding rode hard across the prairie for a quarter mile, then eased off and let his big black walk. He had ridden since he was four. His parents had a big country place on Long Island out of the bustle of New York City. They lived there most of the time, and had a stable of six horses.

When he got in trouble, or was lonely, or mad at everyone, he ran to the stables and rode. Once he was gone two days, riding all the way to the end of Long Island and back. His parents were frantic.

Now he reverted to form. He was angry and mad, he was so damn lonely he could scream. So he rode. He let the big black walk, moving toward the small stream. She drank, then stood in the cool water for a moment before he urged her out to the near bank from the hock deep water.

An hour later he walked the black into the fort just before the noon mess call.

He had worked out the only solution he could. He left his horse with a trooper who hurried up from stable duty and walked into his office, his riding crop slapping steadily on his blue army trousers with the broad yellow stripe down the side.

Lieutenant Riddle looked up from his desk.

"So?"

The captain waved his adjutant into his office and when the door was shut, Harding grinned.

"I'm not taking a company, or a platoon, or even a squad. I'm going out alone, with Big Ear and six of his Tonkawa scouts."

Riddle jolted back a step. "Alone? That's insane, that's . . ." But as he thought about it he began to nod. He laughed softly and then a big grin broke out on his face. "Tricky, but effective. You keep the army out of it. The scouts are on leave, you're on a month's furlough you have coming, and could be in St. Louis, or New Orleans for all we know."

"And I have the best damn protection any soldier ever had. Those Tonks will keep me out of trouble, go around any big band of Comanches, and we will travel light with grass fed Indian ponies. I'll go in buckskins and with my two forty-fours."

"How long, Colt?"

"As long as it takes. I've built up two months of furlough. I'll be leaving tomorrow morning."

"What do I tell Major Zachery?"

"That I'm going on leave to recover from losing my family. The goddamn truth."

"He'll want to inspect your gear before you go – due to his inquiry."

"He's free to do so. Send for Big Ear. I think he'll like the proposition I'm going to make him."

That afternoon Major Zachery interviewed Captain Harding about what he knew of the gold theft. Colt told him exactly what he had done that evening and all that he knew. He told the major that he didn't have the gold or know anything about it, and that he was leaving the next morning on a furlough.

"What about this inquiry?"

"You don't need me here, Major. You can inspect my gear before I leave."

"That won't be required. I did want you here when I find the thief. And I will find him."

"I'm sure you will, Major. Is there anything else?"

Zachery stood, shook his head and walked back to his quarters.

A short time later, Big Ear smiled at the Pony Soldier captain.

"We go long ride. Indian pony. Live Indian style?"

"That's right, quietly, without being seen. We ride until we find which Comanche band has Sadie, and figure how to get her back."

"How pay Big Ear?"

Colt was ready for that. "You know how you've been asking to bring your lodges near the fort? I've decided after this trip, after we find Sadie, then you can bring your tipis and your women and horses to a new camp a mile down from the fort on the river in that little valley."

Big Ear grinned. Colt had a deal. They arranged to meet outside the fort a mile upstream the following morning. Big Ear would bring an extra Indian pony for Colt. He would ride out on an army mount, leave it in the brush and Corporal Swenson would bring it back the next day and slip it back in the corral.

"Tell no one anything about this," Colt cautioned the Tonkawa, but he was certain half the fort would know his arrangements before noon the next day.

Just so it didn't get back to the Division of Texas Headquarters in San Antonio.

Across the compound, Garland Oliver sat on his bed cleaning his army issue .44 Remington pistol. He had his sergeant giving the first platoon riding instruction and drill. The rest of the afternoon was free. He heard a knock on the door, then the partition opened a crack.

"Cleaning lady," a woman's voice said.

Oliver, surprised at first, relaxed. He'd

been jumpy lately, worried about the gold.

"Yes, Mrs. Unru, come in. I'll stay out of your way."

"I could come back later, Lieutenant Oliver."

"No, now is fine."

She smiled, came in, and closed the door. Ellie Unru was not a raving beauty, but out here in the wilds she was a woman and that was enough. She was maybe five feet and three inches, slightly plump and with good breasts. He watched her move around sweeping the plank floor, then dusting and cleaning up some of his equipment that had scattered.

She came toward him and bent to pick up something from the floor. He watched her. As she bent her blouse sagged open and showed both her big breasts hanging free, not encumbered by a wrapper or even a chemise.

She looked up and smiled, but didn't cover herself.

"Well now, I've shown you my . . . my things. Sorry."

"No . . . no, don't move, they are lovely, just beautiful."

She blushed prettily. "Thank you, sir." She hesitated. "Sir, they wouldn't mind getting petted a mite, if you was in the mood and all."

He shot a quick look at her. She was serious. In the six months she'd been cleaning his room, he'd never touched her, even though he'd heard most of the cleaning and laundry women were available with a little persuasion and three dollars.

His hand reached out and pushed inside her blouse, catching one swinging prize.

"I'm in the mood," he said, his voice husky as he hurried to the door and locked it from the inside securely.

A half hour later he lay naked beside Ellie on his bed. She had pulled a blanket up to cover her hips, but her breasts swung free as she sat up.

As he made love to her twice, he had wished he could tell her about the gold. He had made the perfect theft, and now there was no one he could brag about it to! He felt alone and frustrated. He wanted to give Ellie one of the new twenty dollar gold pieces, but knew that would cause him trouble.

Instead he gave her three dollars and she smiled and rubbed her breasts over his face until he chewed on them.

"You're a gentleman, you are," she said. "You make love soft and gentle like the way a woman wants. 'Course I never done nobody on post before, 'cepting my husband. You're a wonder, Lieutenant Oliver, you are."

He kissed her pink nipples again, figured she was about twenty-two or three and helped her dress.

"Ellie, you come again tomorrow to clean, in the afternoon. I want to show you a new game, and I'll have something special to tell you."

She rubbed his crotch through his blue pants.

"You best have something loaded and ready to fire as well," she said, then picked up her cleaning gear, winked at him and went out to the covered porch area and down to the next room she was supposed to clean.

Oliver sat on the bed for a minute, remembering how good it had been with her. Hell, it was *always good* with a woman, better even than in his hand. Sometimes he wondered why he didn't get married so he could have sex every night until he was too weak to get it up.

He laughed and went over and locked his door. He made sure the curtain was covering the narrow window to the courtyard, then he pushed the washstand aside, and using his knife, pried up the loose floor board next to the wall and looked down at the gold.

By now everyone in the fort knew there was eight thousand dollars in gold missing. *Eight thousand in gold!* He picked up a handful of coins. They had the new date on them, 1869. He had no idea when new gold coins went into circulation. But it certainly would be easy to identify these before others of the same minting came out.

He stacked them up, counting out a hundred coins. That was two thousand dollars! He'd never thought he'd have that much cash of his very own. And now he had eight thousand dollars! He must have four hundred of the coins!

Slowly he put the gold back between the two by six joyce below the floor boards. He swung the board back in place and pushed the wash stand so it covered half the four inch wide plank.

He was a rich man!

But he couldn't tell anyone. Perhaps by this time tomorrow he would have a confidant, a woman he could show the gold to, or at least tell her about it, and brag about how he accomplished the feat that had the army brass in convulsions. Yes, tomorrow he would tell Ellie. She would keep his secret. He might even run off with her and the eight thousand dollars.

Oliver stretched out on the bed, daydreaming how pleasant it would be to have Ellie's lush, willing body whenever he wanted to!

Chapter 9

Captain Colt Harding rode out of the fort's unfinished front gate on an army black, not his usual mount since he was going on furlough. His saddlebags were filled with raisins, nuts and all the dried fruit he could find in the storeroom.

In his blanket roll was enough hardtack to keep him and half the Indians coming with him alive for a week. Big Ear had guaranteed his captain that there would be no problem with food. They would hunt as they needed to, they would live off the land.

Colt Harding had left his uniform in his closet. He was not on official business, so he wore a set of well used buckskins he had picked up two years ago in Wyoming.

He was shedding his army image, his army clothes, and soon his army mount. He rode west along the trail to Austin, then when he was out of sight of the fort, cut sharply north to the small stream and found where Big Ear and his men waited.

He had agreed to ride an Indian pony, but held out for a small, light weight saddle. Three of the Tonkawas had saddles. He held up his hand in greeting, then dismounted and moved the saddle off the army black to the smaller, grass fed Indian pony.

Out here the ponies would expect only dry grass and some greenery to eat. There would be no problem finding oats for them.

Big Ear came up and fingered Colt's buckskins.

"From mountains," he said. "You buy far away?"

"Wyoming," Colt said. "Thirty day's long ride west."

That satisfied the leader of the Indian scouts.

Colt had decided to "go Indian." He would take off his buckskin shirt a half hour the first day and let the sun melt into his pale white skin. The second day he would increase the time by fifteen minutes and then fifteen minutes more each day until at the end of the week, he would be able to go all day without the shirt, and he should be a toasted brown. It would let him blend in better with his new detail of fighting men.

His size was a drawback. He knew few Indians who were six feet tall. He would compensate. His only concession to comfort were his army boots, which he hid under the tight legs of his fringed buckskins.

Colt was surprised how fast the Indian

ponies moved across the prairie. They had covered more than fifteen miles when they stopped at a small creek. Two of the Indians vanished into a light sprinkling of woods, and returned in ten minutes with two rabbits and a pair of grouse.

They dressed them out at once, started small fires and soon had them roasted. They pulled the cooked meat apart with their fingers and ate.

Colt did the same thing and while he didn't think he was hungry, the roasted rabbit tasted better than anything he had eaten in a long time.

When the meat was gone, they filled up on water, topped off their army issue canvas water bags, and rode again.

There was no stopping two hours before sun set as Colt was used to with an army unit. Big Ear led the riders, and kept pushing ahead along a trail that would take them well north of the hidden valley and toward the Staked Plains.

They stopped an hour after sunset, and ground tied their horses, then hobbled them and rolled out blankets and slept. Before now, Colt had not been able to understand how the Indians could travel so far across the plains so quickly. He was beginning to get the idea.

They simply punished themselves, riding longer and harder than a Cavalry unit could manage with their heavy stock, heavy equipment, and any wheeled rigs they might have. If he wanted to fight the Indians on an even footing, he would have to make some drastic changes in the way he went about it.

It only took them three days to reach the lofty cap rocks that barricaded their way. They stopped half a mile from the small stream where the band of Comanches had disappeared before.

Big Ear led his men on a series of half circles around the area. Each time they moved closer to the mouth of the small stream and made the circle again. The fourth time, they found hoof prints.

"More than two handsful," Big Ear said. "Indian ponies. None with shoes." He sent one man to scout out the trail the horses had taken once they left the concealment of the small stream. Big Ear went part way down the trail that led generally due east. He pointed to lines in the dust.

"Travois track," he said.

"Which means the women, kids and household gear are all on the move. The band has left the Staked Plains, but in small groups and moving to the east so they can join up at a new location," Colt said, reasoning it out as he went.

Big Ear nodded. He grinned and his eyes almost closed.

"Soup, all right?" he asked.

Colt scowled. What the hell, he was buying friendship and loyalty. Slowly Colt bobbed his head. "Okay for you, not for me. First we have to find the bastards."

"Find bastards, two, three days," Big Ear said.

The following day Big Ear and his remaining men scoured the trails, washes and streams that came down from the high plateau eight hundred feet above. Six places they found where more riders had come away from the Staked Plains. All showed signs of Indian ponies as well as shod stock, and the remains of travois track even after the ponies had been driven over the trail behind the litters.

The Comanches were moving back toward the Brazos.

That night two Tonkawa hunters brought in a small buck deer. It would dress out less than a hundred pounds, but that was still about fifty pounds more meat than they could eat.

To Colt's amazement, the seven Tonks ate an average of six pounds each of the venison the first night. The feast went on for more than six hours, and they rolled away from the fire only when they could stuff no more down their throats.

Colt had not tried to keep up with them, but every hour he had eaten more, and by the end of the evening he felt bloated and groggy. He had been introduced to the Indian law of the plains. Eat when there is food to eat – it may be days before there is anything else.

The following morning the braves rose and staggered away to relieve themselves. When they came back, they uncovered the banked coals of the pit fire, and cooked more venison. It would be rancid by noon. They didn't have time to dry it, so they ate the best portions.

Two hours of feasting and almost all of the venison was gone except the larger bones and some of the tougher meat around the lower legs.

"Now we ride," Big Ear said.

Only then did he tell Colt that one of his men had trailed the Comanche and found where the trails had merged. The main body was more than fifty families, with maybe six hundred head of ponies and horses.

"Should be more horses," Big Ear said. "Maybe come later."

Colt and his Indians reached the juncture trail before six that evening. They followed it until dark, then camped.

Big Ear sent a man on ahead to track the hated Comanche in the moonlight.

Colt had no trouble sleeping. He had total trust in Big Ear. The braves knew that their families back near the fort would suffer if anything happened to the white-eye chief.

With morning, Colt talked to Big Ear.

"Scout come back last night. Comanche camped ten miles ahead, two days ago, then move on. Should catch them in two hard days' ride."

"Chief, we're not a war party. We want to track them, find out where they are and where they might be in two weeks. Then we go back for our forces. Do you understand?"

"You promise soup," Big Ear snapped.

"Would you rather eat soup or live to be an old man with many grandchildren? We are seven against sixty warriors."

Big Ear looked at Colt with anger for a moment, then he smiled and laughed. "Yes, we find now, then later we eat soup. It is good."

The next two days they put fifteen hours in the saddle. Just before dark on the end of the second day, they saw the smokes of the Comanche.

Big Ear and Colt worked up silently to within two hundred yards of the camp. The tipis of the Comanche spread out along the South Fork of the Wichita River. There were more than sixty lodges showing in the bright moonlight. There were no sentries out, no scouts.

The lodges swung around a gentle curve in the Wichita that ran no more than three feet deep now in summer and less than fifty feet wide. The valley had gentle slopes and was a quarter of a mile wide. At once Captain Harding worked out how he would attack the settlement.

Big Ear wanted to go closer, but Colt ordered him back. They moved to their horses and quietly rode away, south and east toward the Fort Comfort.

When they were in the open, Colt took command of the detail. He said they would ride until midnight, sleep until six and ride until they came to the fort.

He relented the next day when it grew dark. But they were halfway. The second day after that they rode into the fort and Harding began immediate preparations for a company sized patrol to go to the field against the Comanche.

Big Ear had seen enough signs and recognized the large tipi that stood at the center of the Indian camp. There was the head of an eagle painted on the tipi cover. It was the Eagle band, the one led by Walking White Eagle, a brilliant, and much loved leader of the Comanche nation.

Chapter 10

The sun rose slowly, as if reluctant to start the new day as it warmed the tipis on the South Fork of the Wichita River in western Texas. The camp came alive slowly. Smoke lifted here and there from the holes in the tops of tipis. Men shuffled into the woods to relieve themselves.

A young boy scampered out of a tipi in his breechclout, threw a rock at a lodge a few yards away and ran quickly to hide behind a tree.

In front of the large tipi with the eagle head on it, White Eagle sat talking with a young brave. He was fifteen, a man-child who was receiving his last instructions before he went on his vision quest.

Every warrior was obliged to go on a vision quest to become a man. He had to talk with Mother Earth alone, live off the bounty of Mother Earth and determine his path in life. It was a pivotal day for Horse Walker, because this was the time he would discover his true medicine and find his warrior name.

It all depended on his vision.

"Horse Walker, you will open your soul to Mother Earth and to all the spirits, you will watch and wait and find your vision before you return. It may only take you a few days, you may be gone for three or four weeks. When you have seen your vision you will know it and you will act as a warrior and say it is time for you to return to your own tipi."

Horse Walker stood, lowered his head in respect, then ran eagerly and vaulted on the back of his war pony still in training. He carried only his personal medicine bag tied between his legs, his breechclout, and his best bow and six arrows. The six arrows indicated he would return before six weeks had passed.

Without looking or speaking to another mortal, Horse Walker rode regally out of camp and into the low hills of the Wichita.

White Eagle smelled the coffee. Of all the gifts of the white-eyes, the coffee bean had been the best, even better than the fire-stick-that-shot-many-times. Always Smiling had roasted the new coffee beans in an iron skillet over a low fire, then mashed them and ground them fine before she scooped them into the copper pot and boiled the coffee.

As he drank the steaming brew, White Eagle toyed with one of the new pistols. He had learned how to take the metal cartridges in and out of the chamber. How to work the hammer. Twice he had fired all six rounds from the weapon.

It had been a thing alive in his hand, and he had to use all of his strength to control it. Not at all like the silent, sturdy feel of a bowstring as it released.

He had taught four of his best warriors how to use the pistol. Had trained them how to shoot it, and how powerful it was. The pistols were to be used only to fight against the Pony Soldiers. It was a condition of his gift and would be absolutely obeyed.

This morning he would train eight more warriors in how to use the pistol. Some of them already had rifles, so it would be easier. The pistols would be the only chance his warriors would have if they were overrun by the blue coats.

The soldiers had fires-many-times pistols, so the Comanche must have them too, so they could defend themselves.

It took all morning to teach the warriors how to load the rounds into the chambers and ready the weapon to fire. They fired until each man had shot his weapon twelve times. Then they loaded them again.

"Keep the fires-many-times pistol with your shield and lance. Keep it loaded always. Be sure no one else touches it, and allow no young boys to be near it. The pistol will be our final defense when fighting with the blue shirted Pony Soldiers."

"It would be good to hunt rabbits with," Running Wolf said.

The men laughed. Running Wolf was not the best marksman with his bow.

"Not hunting. With the pistol we hunt the blue shirts only."

When the session ended, White Eagle walked with Running Wolf back to his tipi and watched Laughing Golden Hair.

She looked more Comanche already. Cries In The Morning had made a proper suede dress for her with fringes of trade beads and some elk's teeth. She had on new, tiny moccasins and her long blonde hair was braided, greased and tied to each side to keep it out of her way.

Sadie sat in the dust in front of the tipi trying to scrape a buffalo hide. She watched Cries In The Morning, and tried to do the same thing with a scraper as big as both her hands. She didn't have the strength yet to do the job.

"*Hi, tai,* little friend," Cries In The Morning said gently. "You will learn. You are trying."

"*Toquet?*" Sadie said looking up. She had learned that word well.

"Yes, you are trying, *toquet*," her Indian mother said.

Sadie turned and stared hard at the tall man. He was the one who hurt Yale and who carried her over his shoulders on the pony. He had hurt her, too. There were still scabs on her wrists where the rawhide had cut into her flesh.

Sadie did not like the tall man. She would never be his friend. She looked back at the hide. The lady beside her with the happy smile, scraped the hide so well. Sadie wanted to do it that good too! She tried again, and again.

White Eagle nodded at the small blonde haired girl and walked back to his tipi. He sat down in front of the big tent, crossed his legs and watched the flow of the life around him.

He had brought the tribal life back into balance. There was a fine edge between too much war and too little, between a band that was falling apart, and one that was growing. The leader had to keep everything in balance, maintain some control, but make the men feel that as a Comanche warrior he was free to join any band he chose.

It had been a mistake to run all the way to

the Staked Plains. The presence of the blue shirts so deep into Comanche lands had sent near panic through the whole band. Never before had the Pony Soldiers penetrated so far into the western lands of his ancestors. Times were changing. The white-eyes kept moving westward. There seemed to be nothing to stop them. They bred like rabbits with a dozen children in each lodge.

White Eagle sighed as he watched the flow of the camp around him. They were back in the plains where the willow grew, where the buffalo were plentiful, where they could find nuts and berries to help make their pemmican more tasty. The first hunt was a good one, the rawhide boxes were heavy with jerky which would be pounded into pemmican for their winter food.

They were on the South Fork of the Wichita, well north of where the Pony Soldiers had found them. Now they were free of the probing eyes and the long rifles of the blue shirts. Now they could get back to the Comanche way of life.

He looked up as Laughing Golden Hair skipped by with a new found friend, a girl a year older. They were chattering and giggling as Laughing Golden Hair tried to learn more Indian words. They hurried past the tipi to the edge of the stream.

The Indian girl pulled off her dress and waded into the stream. Laughing Golden Hair hesitated. The older girl called to her and then the small white girl took off her dress and kicked out of her moccasins and stepped into the cool water. Her skin was tanning slowly. She still was white in contrast to the other children, but soon there were a dozen small girls splashing and laughing and playing water games in the shallow, cool mountain stream.

Talks A Lot came from the tipi with a bowl of nuts and berries for White Eagle. He thanked her and then felt of her swollen belly. She smiled.

"Your son is busy this morning moving to a new camp site I think. He will be a strong son, and will be the new chief when you are eighty winters old!"

White Eagle patted his son again within the womb and sent her on her way. Talks A Lot had been a deliberate effort to sire a son. He must have a son. Talks A Lot had four brothers, and he hoped the idea of males had been strongly rooted in her mind so when her body chose the sex of her child it would be male. He did not understand such things.

The wind and the clouds, the sway of the prairie grass, the way an owl hoots or a crow calls or an eagle screamed all had meaning to

White Eagle. He was a man of the land, a fellow user of the bounty that Mother Earth brought forth.

But when it came to understanding women, he was like a babe trying to fight the People Eaters, the hated Tonkawa. He snorted. Perhaps this time he would have a son. If not he would take a fourth wife. He was a chief, it was not only allowed, but often expected. A son was a necessity for a great chief.

For just a moment he worried about the Pony Soldiers. Who was this blue shirt who worried him? Was he one who had been raided? No, the Comanche never raided a fort or the lodge of a Pony Soldier. They were too strong. An outpost, a small band of the men with yellow stripes up their pants?

Perhaps. Then he remembered the supply train. There had been fifteen blue shirts there. That was where he got the pistols and rifles. The woman and child on the train? Yes, it was possible they had been going to the fort, the family of one of the chiefs? It was a chance.

Perhaps he should put out sentries? Warriors disliked sitting on high points watching a back trail. It was not rightful duty for a real warrior. Tomorrow he would find two or three of the older boys not yet warriors and give them the job of being scouts watching to the south and east. That was where the Pony Soldier wagons had been. That was where the army would come from if they still searched.

He watched four young boys charge through the camp on their ponies. They pretended they were attacking an enemy camp, wielding their short lances, pretending to shoot with their bows as they maneuvered their ponies through the crowded camp using only their knees and feet. They were developing the skills they would need as warriors.

For a moment he was at peace, pleased with his band, happy that his son was growing and would be born in a month. Satisfied with the first hunt for their winter's food.

In a month it would be time to go meet the Mexican traders, who had beads and mirrors and all sorts of steel and metal they could fashion into arrow and lance points. They traded for horses and mules. On the next raid he would keep his stolen horses for trading.

White Eagle stood up and went inside his big tipi. He found his second wife Prairie Flower who sat in her raised bed sewing on a pair of heavy winter leggings for him.

Gently he curved his hand around her breast. She glanced up eagerly, dropped her sewing and held his hand to her breast. He sat beside her. Quickly she lay down lifting the soft suede dress she wore.

"Today I think it is right so I can make a fine son for you, White Eagle. I so much want to bear you a son!"

White Eagle rolled on top of her and nibbled at her ear lobe.

A few minutes later, he did the best he could, planting his seed deeply into her. The rest was up to Prairie Flower.

Outside again, he called to the three young boys and gave them their lookout assignments. They accepted them with anticipation. It was a first step to becoming a warrior, and it meant there might be trouble and a chance to prove their valor in battle! They took a few provisions with them, got their bows and arrows, and raced for their ponies. They would not be back for five days, the usual time for a lookout.

They were almost warriors, defending their families, and the whole camp. It would be a wonderful adventure!

White Eagle watched them go, remembering his first call to be a lookout when he was twelve. He had watched for raids by the People Eaters. One had come and he had hurried to warn the camp, then been in the heat of the battle.

That day he had taken his first scalp. He had become a full fledged warrior when he was thirteen.

White Eagle sat near his shield and lance in front of his tipi and thought about earlier days. Why did things have to change? Why were the Pony Soldiers chasing them?

Chapter 11

Major Zachery was the second man to see Captain Harding after he returned from his long range scouting trip. He scowled with disapproval as Colt signed some forms on his desk and cleaned up the paper work he had missed while he was gone.

"Captain, that was a foolhardy thing you did, chasing off after those savages."

"I found them, Major, that's the important factor."

"No, Harding, the important fact is that we still haven't recovered the eight thousand in gold that belongs to the United States Army. I want the matter settled before you go on this patrol."

"Do you have all of your interviews conducted yet?"

Major Zachery turned away. "No, not all of them."

"Then I'd suggest that would be the most crucial part of the investigation. I'll be glad to leave any men here you need to talk to."

"When are you leaving?"

"In two days at the most. I don't want White Eagle to move his band again."

"I'll give you a list of men I need to talk to."

"Good. Now if you'll excuse me, Major, I have a fight to get ready for. No longer am I chasing Indians. I'm finding them, waiting for them, then attacking them for a goddamn change!"

Ten minutes later Lieutenant Riddle scratched his balding head and looked in wonder at the orders.

"I don't understand. No sabers, no bugle, no wagons, no pocket change, and each man to carry his own rations for fourteen days?"

"You read well, John. Damn well."

"Living off the land?"

"Half the time, until we get beyond a certain point. The Indians will be given the same rations, but will act as hunting providers. We'll make out fine."

John Riddle tossed down his pencil and snorted. "I could fix you up with Indian ponies too, if you want. Then you wouldn't have to carry any oats."

"I'd love that, but we don't have time to train the troops. I'm the only one besides the Tonkawas who'll be on an Indian pony. Those little nags are used to grass feed. They can move sixty miles a day without even breathing hard."

"You're serious?"

"Damn right. Remember I just came back from a long ride on one of those little grass eating wonders." He took a list from his pocket. "We'll take B company this time. Make sure none of the men on that list are used as fillers. Major Zachery still needs to talk to them."

"Easy, compared to what you're going to do. Two weeks with no wagon support?"

"We'll turn the Indian tactic against him. We move fast, and as quietly as possible. No gunfire of any kind allowed before contact with the hostiles. All hunting will be by bow and arrow. We'll travel light, push our mounts to their limit, sleep in the open without tents, cut down every pound of weight we can. The less the horses have to carry, the faster and farther we can move every day.

"If the damn Comanches can make sixty miles a day, then Company B and I damn well can too!"

The following day, Company B with six fillers from Company A, mounted up for inspection. They were lean and trim. They carried one blanket per man, ten pounds of oats, no shelter half or ground cloth, no change of boots or uniform, no sabers, and no extra food, just the fourteen days' ration.

"Feels like we're going on a damn picnic!" one of the troopers yelped.

Captain Harding himself made the inspection. The troops had been ordered to tie their blanket roll in front of the saddle as usual, and to tie the bag of grain immediately behind their saddle where the tent half usually rested. Their food supply would be in their saddlebags, or tied in back with the grain.

Half way through the inspection, the captain turned it over to Lieutenant Edwards, the B Company Commander.

"You know what I want, Edwards. Any weight we can save will give us that much more advantage."

In his quarters, Garland Oliver relaxed after a day of drilling his company. When their chance came, he wanted them to be experts on horseback and with their weapons.

Now he looked over his "rich" list. He still hadn't decided what he would do, or when with his brand new eight thousand in gold. He had an idea it would be a good practice simply to take the gold and two good horses from the stables, and vanish some night just after taps. In short, to desert. He'd have a good twelve hour head start and with two horses to trade off, he could be well toward Austin before they could send anyone after him.

His plans for escape were interrupted by a knock on the door. Ellie Unru came in with fresh towels and a bucket filled with all sorts of cleaning materials. Once inside she set down the items and flew into Oliver's arms. They fell on the bed and tickled each other and then quickly undressed and began to pet and stroke each other.

Before she let him enter her she smiled sweetly.

"First, promise that you'll show me the gold. You said you would, now I want your promise as an officer and a gentleman." He lunged at her but she moved her hips and they both laughed.

"I promise, I promise, before you go today, I'll show you the gold."

She smiled and opened her knees, accepting him.

They made love furiously, twice, and then she dressed quickly and looked at him. She stood aside while he moved the washstand and lifted the floor board. He gave her two of the gold pieces and watched her expression. As she fondled them he fondled her breasts and she smiled and kissed him.

"We're going to have a wonderful life together, Garland. There's my husband of course, but he won't mind. He's all army anyway. We'll just leave him here when we run away together."

She kissed him again, rubbed his crotch and then slipped out the door with her cleaning gear heading for the next quarters to work on.

The next morning at six A.M., B Company rode out from Fort Comfort, Texas under the command of Captain Harding, with Lieutenant Edwards and Lieutenant Ned Young and ninety-five enlisted men.

The first day they made a little over fifty miles. The men grumbled as they kept riding into twilight, and didn't stop an hour after dark. Usually a cavalry unit stopped two hours before sunset. They cooked their salt pork ate it with hardtack and swilled it down with coffee before they fell into their blankets.

It was the usual 4:45 A.M. rising, but there was no bugle. The captain's orderly roused each sergeant who kicked his men out of blankets. They were in the saddle by 5:30, a half hour early, and again the men voiced their displeasure.

The Tonkawas were along in force, twenty-three of them, and all eager to draw some Comanche blood, and if possible eat some Comanche soup. They all knew what they had been promised by the white-eyes captain. For most of the Tonkawas any excuse to kill a Comanche was valid.

The second day the Indians brought in a dozen rabbits and ten grouse. While not enough meat for all the troops, half of them had meat that night, with the other half in line for meat the next day.

The second day Harding and his tough little Indian Pony, with Big Ear at his side, churned up a little more than sixty miles by the captain's calculations. It was an hour and a half after sunset when the first cooking fires blossomed in a stretch of brush along one of the many rivers that run east and west through northwestern Texas.

Neither Harding nor Big Ear knew which one it was. They did know they were half way to the Comanche camp on the South Fork of the Wichita.

That night, Harding and Edwards went over the layout of the bend in the Wichita where White Eagle had camped.

"We'll put half our troops at each end of the camp, if we can take them by surprise," Harding said. "Then on a gunshot signal, we drive toward the center, and force anyone who runs to go across the water to the other side. The stream will slow them down."

"We shoot just the braves, Captain?"

Harding set his jaw. "Lieutenant, have you ever seen a cabin or a ranch or a wagon train when the Comanche get through with it?"

"No sir."

"They kill everything that breathes, everything! We'll repay them in kind. But – no children. Make it clear to your men that the braves and squaws are targets, but no children. My baby girl is in that camp somewhere, and I'm going to tear every lodge apart until I find her!"

"Yes sir. Understood. Not a single child will be hurt, no exceptions."

Captain Harding walked around the small campfire they had, then stared off into the distance, north and a little west. His Sadie was up there somewhere, and he was coming to take her home!

The third day of the march the men were tired and sore. None of them had ever traveled a hundred and ten miles in two days before. The fact that they were only half way to the battle cut at them as they rode.

But they kept moving. They were heading into a battle! Most of them had never faced an Indian. Some of the men had been on the frontier for three years and chased dozens of Indian Bands but never caught one. Now they would see the sight of blood.

They stopped for a scheduled cold noon break. They rubbed down their horses, watered them and were about to start again when four Tonkawa scouts came into the group with two freshly killed deer.

Captain Harding gave the word and the troops fell to butchering the deer and cooking it. Most of the meat wound up fried in skillets over quickly made fires. Within an hour the two deer had been reduced to a pile of bones as the troopers each had a slap of venison.

Morale was much better the rest of the afternoon and two hours of riding into the night before they made camp. Most of the men still bloated with venison, ignored supper, rolled up in their blankets and slept.

The next day at noon, Big Ear welcomed back two advance Tonk scouts who reported that there were lookouts on the trail ahead. The scouts had caught sight of the lookouts when they flashed mirrors at each other in the bright sunlight.

"Locate them all, then eliminate them quietly," Captain Harding said. "We want to be a total surprise to the main camp."

The main party rested at four that afternoon in a heavy stand of timber at what Big Ear said was three miles from the Comanche lodges.

Big Ear and Captain Harding moved up through the small hills and underbrush until they could look down on the tipis spread along the small river.

"Somewhere down there is my baby girl," Harding whispered half to himself. He would find her. Damned if he wouldn't!

Back at the main party, Harding ordered that there would be no talking above a whisper. The men were to cook their supper and turn in. They would be up at three A.M. to move into attack position.

The grumbling ceased, as men began to sweat. Most faced a battle for the first time in their lives. The blooded veterans knew the risks, and fell into the habit that they had built up before any battle. Some wrote letters. Some read letters. A few prayed. All of them turned and twisted trying to go to sleep.

At 3:30 A.M., Company B moved silently through the light brush. Half the troop under Lieutenant Edwards, two platoons, swung to the north. Captain Harding and forty-five men of Platoons Three and Four were at the southern end of the half mile long Indian campsite.

Captain Harding kept his troops mounted and a hundred yards behind a low crest. Just over the ridgeline, a gentle slope ran another hundred yards to the first sprinkling of Comanche tents.

The day before the sun had risen at 5:30. Today should be about the same Colt figured. They would attack as soon as it was light enough to see, a few minutes after dawn, maybe 5:10. He checked his six-guns, both were firmly in place.

His signal shot, when it came, would be from his Spencer repeating rifle, and the round would tear into the big tipi with the eagle on it. Big Ear had told the captain that most likely the chief, White Eagle, had brought back the girl child to be adopted by a woman with no child. So Sadie would not be in the chief's tent.

The morning began to lighten.

A bird called its morning song.

Somewhere a coyote wailed its last lonesome plea for a mate.

Captain Harding looked at the tipis below. It was time!

He lifted his rifle over his head and brought it down to the front. The troopers behind him walked their mounts forward, in a platoon front, stretched out in a line forty-five men wide. When they were in position, he raised the Spencer again, and this time sent two rounds into the largest Tipi.

His men surged forward, silently. The hooves made almost no noise on the soft floor of the woodsy slope.

There had been no answering shot from the northern point, there was not supposed to be.

Captain Harding rode silently ahead of the others, then fell back in line, so some eager marksman didn't shoot him instead of a Comanche.

A tent flap flew upward and a surprised Comanche warrior stepped outside his lodge. Two rounds from carbines slammed into his chest, driving him into his own happy hunting ground inside his tent.

A woman screamed.

From the northern part of the camp came more rifle fire.

Here a dozen flaps came up, braves slipped out, doubled over, running toward the horses. Some brought up rifles and returned fire.

The charging troopers fired at anyone who moved, smashed into the tipi area before many of the Indians managed to get outside.

Captain Harding dropped the reins of his Indian pony, brought up both pistols and fired at a brave just leaving a lodge. The round caught him in the throat killing him instantly. The captain flashed past the lodge, came to a second one where most of the Indians were out, the men, women and children running toward the river.

Harding charged forward, knocked down the squaw and shot the brave through the back. He looked anxiously at the three children racing for the stream. None of them was Sadie, too large and too dark haired.

He whirled the Indian pony, saw his men methodically firing into the lodges, chasing anyone who left them.

Directly ahead of Captain Harding a brave ran from a tipi, in his hand an army revolver. Harding bellowed in rage and shot the Indian twice in the chest, then charged over him with the Indian pony and stormed toward the next knot of frightened Indians.

To the north, Edwards' men swept everything in front of them as they worked forward. Half a dozen women and children shied into the river, rushed across and vanished in the brush on the far side.

Two braves darted and stumbled and scurried through the horses and tipis to the fringe of woods and slid in out of sight.

Edwards slashed a warrior with his saber, lopping off his ear and severing the left carotid artery. The brave died before he slid to the ground.

The men of Company B concentrated on the braves, but now and then a squaw would come in their sights and they fired. Nobody tried to kill any children but some fell under the hooves of the prancing, charging mounts.

Two minutes after the first shots were fired the confused mass of men, horses, women and children was unbelievable. The troopers hardly knew who to fire at. Blue shirts were on every side and they reverted to their pistols for quick, sure shots.

Woman and children splashed through the stream and into the safety of the woods on the far side. It quickly became obvious to the Indians that the Pony Soldiers were not following them there. They located children and relatives and hurried farther away to safe hiding places in thick brush.

Only two braves made it to their horses, and both were dispatched by rifle fire before they could get within fighting range with their lances, the only weapon they had time to snatch up as they ran through the melee.

Warriors concentrated on saving their lives. They had no weapons with which to fight, they were totally surprised, many running around naked from their beds.

Half the warriors who were given pistols caught them up and used them. Running

Wolf killed one Pony Soldier and seriously wounded a second before three of the Cavalrymen saw him with the weapon and cut him down with a dozen shots. He fell between tipis and was trampled a dozen times by charging army mounts.

Captain Harding suffered a bullet wound to the left shoulder. He kept riding and firing, reloading his right handed weapon twice before he looked around and saw that the braves who could still fight had been driven away. Those left were so wounded they couldn't move.

For a terrible few moments there were a dozen pistol shots as badly wounded Indians and horses were put out of their misery.

Captain Harding took casualty reports from his officers. They had suffered four dead, twelve wounded. Two of the Tonkawas had been killed, but Edwards was not sure if they were shot by the Comanche or his own men.

As he watched, Harding saw two Tonks slipping off into the brush. Each carried something. The captain was not sure he wanted to know what it was.

He had his men form up and they went through the village tipi by tipi, looking for one small blonde girl. They did not find her. Over the half mile stretch there were more than twenty bodies. When the final count was made of the enemy losses, Captain Harding nodded grimly.

They had found twelve dead braves, six women and two young boys. The Tonkawa scouts had killed three youths on the lookout posts. Twenty-three dead. It was a good start.

Now they would burn everything in the village.

Even as he thought of it, a cold wind sprang up and ten minutes later, a crashing thunderstorm struck, sending lightning flashes by the dozen, thunder rolling almost continually, and a slashing wind driven rain that pushed the Pony Soldiers inside the lodges for shelter.

Most were amazed how well made the tipis were, and how well they turned aside the rain.

"Looks damn like the cabin where I grew up, 'cepting it's round," one rawboned recruit drawled.

When the storm had passed a half hour later, Captain Harding decided everything was too wet to burn. Instead he sent his men in two waves into the brush across the river looking for the Indian women and children, and his daughter.

He led the probes. They discovered two small groups of Indian women and kids, but there was no child there the right age, let alone with blonde hair and blue eyes.

Harding let them go and rode back to the village, where he tied his dead over their saddles, replaced two dead army mounts with Indian ponies and tied two of the dead men on board.

He had twelve men injured. Only one who shouldn't be riding, but there was no other way to get home. For a moment Harding considered using one of the Indian travois, but he quickly rejected the idea. No self respecting Cavalryman would lay on that contraption for two hundred miles. He'd rather be dead.

He put out security and let Corporal Marlin take care of the wounded. He poured some liquid on the captain's shoulder wound, then bound it tightly.

"The slug went right on through, sir. We're lucky there. Got a few that didn't. If we can get home in five days, should be all right." It took two hours to get the wounded ready to travel.

Captain Harding was a mile away from the Eagle band camp when he realized that none of the Tonkawa braves were with him. He had promised them soup, so they were having it. There was no way he could stop them. He was sure by now their soup was boiling and it would be supplemented with fried steaks.

The Tonkawas were indeed the People Eaters as the other Indians said. But they were also the best scouts that Captain Harding had.

He guessed that the Tonks would rejoin the line of march sometime the following day.

They did, arriving at noon, sliding into place as if they had never been away. The only difference Harding could notice was a sly smile that Big Ear now carried, and he moved quickly when Harding spoke.

It would be a long ride back to Fort Comfort. Harding knew he had failed. He had ridden the Comanche to ground, he had attacked him on his own territory, in his own village, but he had not found Sadie. The report to the Division of Texas would be one of victory, but in his heart he knew the one victory he wanted had not happened.

He would return. He would find the Eagle band again, and when he did, he would watch and wait. He would make sure where his daughter was being held prisoner, which woman had adopted her, and then he would strike in the night with a swift and sure scalpel, cutting out the one tipi, moving inside quietly and finding his daughter, killing everyone there and slipping away like an avenging angel in the night before anyone knew he had been there.

Yes! That was how he would find his

daughter, how he would rescue her. He still owed the damned Comanche more than he could ever repay. Today's fight was simply an interest payment against the principal. He couldn't wait to go after the hostiles again, as soon as possible.

It had to be before winter. Until then he would have to play soldier at the fort. He had to make it all look like a regular Cavalry Post functioning the way it should.

He could play the game. He had to. At least until he found Sadie.

Chapter 12

Cries In The Morning had been awake that fateful morning, watching her small golden haired daughter sleeping. It was a delight for her to look at the child any time of the day, no matter what she was doing. She got up and made sure the buffalo robe was around the small pale shoulders, then stood and looked at her husband.

At the same moment she heard the report of the rifle and the slugs hitting the big tipi nearby. She knew at once that it meant they were being attacked by the Pony Soldiers.

She grabbed Laughing Golden Hair from the buffalo robes, held her tightly and ran to the flap of the tipi.

Cautiously she lifted it a crack and peered out. On the hill across the way she saw a line of blue coated Pony Soldiers riding forward and firing their long guns.

She screamed at her husband. He was on his feet already, searching for his pistol.

Cries In The Morning knew the white-eyes must never see her golden child or they would take her back. She slipped out the flap, edged around her lodge and ran past two others toward the stream. It was the only way to go. She could hear firing from the other end of the camp. There were Pony Soldiers there as well.

Laughing Golden Girl did not make a sound. Her eyes were as big as the new moon. Her small arms clung to Cries In The Morning as she splashed into the stream, waded up to her waist across the deepest part and then rushed up the far bank and into the fringe of trees and brush.

Cries In The Morning hurried into the deeper woods and found a thorn thicket. She lay down and holding Laughing Golden Hair she slowly worked her way under the thorns a dozen feet into the center of the maze, where she found room enough to sit up.

Gingerly she broke off the dead stalks, and then remembered her knife strapped to her ankle. She used it to cut away more of the thorns until they had an easy place to sit.

Cries In The Morning could hear the screams, the rifle shots, the cries of a horse that was wounded. She told Laughing Golden Hair to stay where she was.

"I must go and help the others," she said, then held out both hands with palms flat and pushed them toward Sadie.

At last Sadie nodded, *"Toquet,"* she said softly. Cries In The Morning nodded and wormed her way out the way she had come in. Now she didn't have to hold the child and it was much easier.

She peered from the thorn bush. She saw no one. Cries In The Morning lifted up and ran toward the river. At the edge of the brush she saw a dozen women she knew, some crying, some with children. She saw one woman floating face down in the water, drifting slowly downstream.

The camp was a mass of terror, battle and confusion. Nowhere did she see the brave warriors putting up a fight. They had been totally surprised. Most had been still in bed. She could not see Running Wolf.

The Pony Soldiers were everywhere, trampling down tipis, riding through drying racks, shooting at both men and women. She saw one warrior leave the place they had the horses, but he was shot and dropped off his mount.

Tears streamed down her face. So many were dying! There must be something she could do! She saw Prairie Flower struggling through the water. There was blood on her chest!

Cries In The Morning leaped up and ran as fast as she could to the edge of the stream, splashed in and waded to Prairie Flower. She caught the young woman's shoulders and urged her through the water to the far bank.

Prairie Flower fell there, and Cries In The Morning talked to her softly, told her they had to move farther, to get out of sight.

"Just a few more steps, help me get you to safety!" Cries In The Morning said. The woman she tried to lift did not respond. She lay as if she were unconscious.

Cries In The Morning lifted her head and turned her over. The stain on her chest had stopped bleeding. The pump that pushed the blood through her veins had stilled. Her eyes stared at the sky without seeing how blue and beautiful it had been moments before.

Cries In The Morning lay Prairie Flower's head down gently, turned and looked for others she could help. She caught a baby from a woman who already had one to carry and they raced into the woods.

Cries In The Morning made a dozen trips into the water. She had seen quickly that the Blue Shirts were not firing at those in the stream. She helped them up the bank and into the woods, and urged them to run deeper into the woods and hide themselves so the Pony Soldiers would not be able to find them.

She lay at the fringe of the woods, her breath coming in ragged gasps. There were no more to come across. The rest were dead or captured. She had recognized the war cries of the Tonkawa. She had not seen any of the hated People Eaters, but she knew they must be in the fighting. The very thought made her shiver. Now, with nothing more to do, she hurried back to the briar growth, found the same spot and wormed her way inside where her Laughing Golden Hair reached for her, holding her tight.

"I didn't think you were ever going to come back!" Sadie Harding yelped in sudden pain and spoke in English. She cried then, cried because this reminded her of when the guns had fired before and her brother was hurt and her mother was thrown out of the wagon. It all hurt so much. She never wanted to see anything like that again.

When the first bullets struck his lodge,

Walking White Eagle came alert at once. The sound of the gun was enough to tell him they were under attack. He uttered a fierce war cry of the eagle, grabbed his bow and six arrows and his pistol and slid out the flap of his tent slowly. His tipi was near the center of the half mile string. He yelled at two or three other braves who joined him.

They could hear the firing now at both ends of the camp. They all headed away from the river, toward the high ground immediately in front of the tipis, but not yet covered by the Pony Soldiers. Three more warriors joined them so they were seven. They ran like antelope, squirming past the first twenty yards of open ground before the Pony Soldiers worked down to them.

Once in the cover of the trees they moved to the north, in behind the Pony Soldiers and sent a dozen arrows at the attackers. One Pony Soldier went down, but they rapidly moved out of range.

Two of the warriors with White Eagle had pistols, but they were no good at this range. He waved the party of six warriors forward. They crawled on their bellies the last fifty yards, sprang up directly behind the Pony Soldiers and at twenty yards fired into a half dozen men who were racing around a tipi, terrorizing a woman and two children inside.

One of the Pony Soldiers fell dead, a second was wounded before the blue shirts turned their fire at the warriors. Each of the soldiers had a pistol and they all rode hard at the seven warriors, knocking down one and scattering the rest.

White Eagle was out of ammunition. He had shot his last arrow. His attack was over. He could do nothing now but watch his beloved band be ravaged by the Pony Soldiers. Tears crept down his cheeks as he watched. He should charge into the melee with his knife, but he knew he would die quickly. There must be a hundred of the mounted men. Only one or two of his band had made it to a war pony.

White Eagle hung his head in shame. What happened to the lookouts? Why hadn't they been warned the soldiers were coming?

Then he saw a flash of Pony Soldiers below and three Tonkawa braves rode by as the fighting quickly died to an occasional burst of pistol fire.

The battle was over, the Eagle band had lost. Now all he could hope for was that the officers would not order everything destroyed. He could not even get across the river now and help protect the women and children who were driven that way.

What did this white-eye chief want? Why

had he used Comanche tactics against the Comanche? He had used surprise. He had hired Tonkawas to scout and kill the lookouts. He had raided the Comanche in his heartland, his summer camp, the very soul of the Comanche nation.

How was this white-eye chief so smart? He must be part Comanche to think like a Comanche.

White Eagle had to lie in his hiding place as the Pony Soldiers scoured the far bank and into the woods hunting for something. He never did figure out what. When they captured a group of women and children the soldiers simply looked at them, shook their heads and let the captives go free.

So the white-eye chief wasn't quite good enough to be a Comanche, or he would never have let the captives go.

Two hours later the wounded Pony Soldiers were mended, their dead loaded on horses and the troop moved out of the camp. The hard thunder shower may have convinced them that Mother Earth was not pleased with the Pony Soldiers. It also made everything so wet they failed to burn the first tipi they tried to light on fire.

Another half hour and the column moved out of camp, four wide, riding as though they were on a parade, moving away from the destruction, the death. Using rear guards and pickets along the sides.

White Eagle watched and learned. He also noticed that the People Eaters were not with the Pony Soldiers. His eyes hardened as he realized where the Tonkawas were, and what they were doing.

As soon as it was safe, he sent the four warriors he had around him to round up the rest, to bring everyone still alive to the hill beyond the river, where they could assemble. He rushed to the place where the boys herded the horses.

The stock had not been bothered. He whistled for Flying Wind who came at once. He rode to a high point where he could see the way south. The column of blue shirts was now three miles away and proceeding. He would send out scouts to check their march.

Next he rode to the Street Of Tears, and checked each of the dead.

Already he could hear the keening and the wailing of the mourners. He found two young warriors, told them to go get their war ponies and follow the Pony Soldiers until they stopped for their night camp, then come tell how far away they were.

He assembled the rest of the band. Twenty lay dead in the camp. He feared the three lookouts would be found dead and mutilated.

It was a severe blow.

Twelve warriors had been killed. He called the remains of the council around him on the hill and they decided what they must do. First the bodies would be prepared for the burial rites, then the camp would be struck and moved far from this river of death.

Suvate! This place was finished. Never again would a Comanche band camp here winter or summer.

Always Smiling sought out White Eagle and told him of Prairie Flower's death. He walked to where she lay and dropped to his knees and cried. There was nothing he could say. She had been a good wife, she had borne him a daughter. He would always remember her. He could stay near her only a short time. He had the whole camp's welfare to think about.

He carried her across the river and put her on her bed in the tipi. Then he counted the dead and wept.

By midday all of the People still alive had returned to the camp. Six of the tipis were ruined beyond repair. Only parts of the buffalo skins could be used in a new tipi cover. The lodges were taken down, everything that could be salvaged was saved and packed and an hour after high sun, they were on the march, northward. But there was no joy, no laughter, no rambunctious boys tearing around.

It was a journey of tears.

They wound as high into the hills as they could get. Then carried the bodies of their dead to the highest point and wedged them into crevices of rocks where their spirits could be free to float into the heavens.

There was only enough time for the briefest of burial ceremonies. The three lookouts had been found and brought back to the camp by warriors. They were buried in the same ceremony.

Then White Eagle pushed the People northward again. They were nearly out of their traditional territory. It couldn't be avoided. They would push into the fringes of the Kiowa territory and try to go around any Kiowa camps they saw. White Eagle hoped they could find a good camp on one of the forks of the Red River.

He worried about the twelve lodges without warriors. Cries In The Morning lost her husband. How would she live? White Eagle sought her out and soon the arrangement was made. Cries In The Morning and Laughing Golden Hair would come to his lodge. Her tipi would be given to one of the warriors who had lost his in the raid when horses drove their hooves through it in a dozen places and tore and ripped it into pieces.

Cries In The Morning would not be his wife, she would be an aunt, do her share of the work, and White Eagle would hunt for her and the child and support them. In turn she would care for the daughter of Prairie Flower.

All around the line of march, other arrangements were being made. Two of the widows went back to their parents' lodge to live. Two others found a brother who would take them in until they could marry again.

The ruined tipis would be replaced as soon as possible. At least the white-eyes had not burned their robes and lodges, or scattered and burned their jerky ready to be made into pemmican. The raid had been costly, but not shattering. Their lives would go on, but there were wounds that would never heal, dead who would never return, and dreams and plans forever lost.

White Eagle looked at the campsite Always Smiling had picked out for them. They had been on the move for five days. They had crossed one branch of the Red River and moved farther north and west to another one. Again they were in the northern fringes of the traditional lands of the Comanche.

This would be a good camp site. It had water, and graze for the herds. Plenty of firewood. At once he began to think how it could be defended. Where he would want his scouts and lookouts. Never again would he sit in his lodge fat and happy and not worry. He had twenty souls on his conscience.

From now, forever more, he would be at war with the white-eyes. They would not catch him sleeping again. The white-eye Pony Soldier chief who led the raid on his camp would know sorrow, he would know pain.

White Eagle would discover who the Pony Soldier was. He had yellow stripes down his legs as the chiefs did, and he carried two revolvers in holsters around his waist. Once he had seen the man plainly. The two revolvers had white handles. There should be someone among the tribes who had heard of this Pony Soldier chief. White Eagle would find his name and one day they would meet on the field of battle and one of them would die!

Chapter 13

Captain Colt Harding rode with his men into Fort Comfort the sixth day away from the hostiles. There was no rush to get back. He had extracted a heavy price from the Comanche, but he had paid with the lives of four of his men.

He took a long hot bath. Had his orderly, Corporal Swenson, order him a steak dinner with mashed potatoes and all the trimmings from the cooks, then he faced Major Zachery. The sour look on the officer told the captain what he wanted to know.

"No luck yet in finding your gold, I see."

Major Zachery stared at Harding for a moment, then sat down in the chair beside the desk.

"None. I've got a pair of suspects, but no evidence." He frowned for a moment. "Captain, the sooner we get this solved, the quicker you get me off your post."

"Hell, Major, you're welcome to stay as long as you want to. Looks like my promotion got hung up again. Place this size should have a major or two around."

"I may retire right here. Captain Harding, I've got two of your men who are smart enough, and who had certain opportunity to make the theft. They could have stolen the gold and are just sitting on it. Not a single one of those coins have showed up in the fort sutler's cash box. It takes a special kind of man to hold eight thousand dollars in his hands, and not spend even one of those double eagles."

"Like who?"

"Corporal Ingles, for one. He's an old hand, plenty smart enough, clever and he had more opportunity than anyone else."

"Not a chance on Ingles. He's been in my command for almost three years. Who else?"

"Lieutenant Oliver."

"Now there, you might have something. He's certainly capable, but you do need one little item like evidence. Have you searched his quarters?"

"He's smart enough not to keep the gold there, if he has it. I'm waiting, hoping he'll slip up."

"I wish you luck. He's smart, too smart sometimes. Maybe when I get my reports done on this patrol, I can give you some help?"

Major Zachery waved. "Not much use right now. I'm going to relax and try to beat Dr. Jenkins in our nightly chess game."

When he left Harding leaned back in his chair. His patrol strike at the Comanche had issued his challenge. He would ride the Comanche into the dust if he could. He wasn't sure how many bands there were roaming western Texas, but it was not a large tribe, maybe seven or eight hundred.

He went to his map and put a spot of red

ink on the south fork of the Wichita where he had hit the Eagle band. From now on he would question every scout, every trader, every traveler he could about the Comanche. Soon he hoped he would have another chance at the Eagle band.

In his quarters across the way, Lieutenant Oliver had come back from the officers' mess, feeling full of good food and satisfied with himself. Timing, that's all it was now. He could have taken off when Captain Harding was away on patrol, but it didn't feel right. It would have to be soon.

Ellie was getting to be a pest. Now that she knew about the gold she kept asking him when they were running away. He certainly wasn't going to take her, but that would have to be a surprise for her the day he left.

A knock sounded on the door and the knob turned. He had forgotten to lock it from the inside. Ellie stepped in quickly and closed the door. She had a pair of clean towels over her arm and she dropped them on his bed.

"You locked me out this afternoon. Why you lock me out? Ain't I good enough for you all of a sudden?"

"Ye gods, woman, I was tired. You've been servicing me every day for two weeks. A man gets enough for a time."

"Not you, you're always ready." She did a

slow strip tease and soon was naked standing in front of him. She pushed one of her big breasts into his mouth and he groaned and pulled her over on his bed.

After they made love, she asked to see the gold again. He hadn't showed it to her since the first night.

"It's still there, don't worry. It's the best hiding spot I can think of."

"So show me again. I want to touch it, to feel it!"

He opened the floor board and she let the twenty dollar gold pieces fall through her fingers.

"That feels so good!" She turned to him. Neither of them had dressed yet. "I've been making plans. I'm going to Austin to visit my great aunt next week. It's all planned. I'll ride in the empty wagons going back to Austin. I've got permission and all. That will be a fine time for you to meet me in Austin and we'll ride north as fast as we can heading for St. Louis!"

"I can't go. I have a three day patrol starting tomorrow. I'm taking fifteen men on a scouting patrol. We go out once a month."

"Oh, damn! I had counted on it. Maybe I should cancel my visit to my great aunt."

"I think you should."

He took the gold from her hands, dropped

it back in the hole and closed the floor boards.

"I also don't think you should come here again for at least a week. Somebody is bound to notice when you come so often."

"I sell my cunt, everybody on post knows it."

"Still, I'm under suspicion by the major. Just don't come around for a week."

"You dumping me over?"

"Of course not, we've got an arrangement. I just need another two or three weeks."

He kissed her, rubbed her breasts and then between her legs and she lost her pout.

"One more quick one?"

He shook his head. "I've got a chess game down at the sutler's. But it is a nice idea." He got rid of her at last, closed his quarters and locked them this time and did go to the sutler's for a bottle of beer and a chess game if he could find one.

A day later the sweep patrol left the fort with fifteen men under the command of Lieutenant Oliver. It was not the best duty, and he was still smarting that he had made three of them in a row now, but he went without any obvious rancor.

Ellie Unru watched the troops go, as did a few of the Pony Soldiers. It was a patrol full of hard riding, no danger but a lot of discomfort.

Ellie gave the patrol four hours to get away from the fort, so she was sure they wouldn't return. She cleaned the two rooms next to Oliver's then tried his door. It was locked. She used a key from her ring, a skeleton key that would open any of the simple door locks, and slipped inside.

She wasted no time. First she threw the bolt on the door behind her, went directly to the washstand and pushed it aside. With a knife, she lifted the floor boards and stared down at the gold.

She had left everything but essentials out of her cleaning bucket. Now she put the gold coins in the bottom of the bucket and lifted it. Yes, she could carry it, but it took both hands.

She made sure she got the last coin, then put the board back and pushed the wash stand over it.

She smiled as she rubbed the gold.

Ellie knew she was the richest woman in sixteen counties!

She put her cleaning things on top of the gold, covering it completely with a cloth, then carried the heavy bucket to the door.

Ellie knew she could not go directly back to her quarters. She had to do the rest of her work. She had two more officer rooms to clean.

She went outside, locked the door behind her, and carried the bucket with both hands fifty feet to the next officer's room. She had trouble getting the job done inside, and she admitted it was not a complete cleaning. She was so excited she could hardly keep from wetting her drawers! She owned eight thousand dollars in gold! It was almost too much to understand. She would have to get used to it a little at a time.

She did one more room, then carried the bucket back to her quarters where the eight married enlisted men were housed. Once inside she tried to think of a spot to hide the gold. Oliver would know who took it at once.

Every hiding place she figured out she later rejected. It had to be outside, she decided at last. And she had to bury it in a bucket, but that meant she had to do it after dark. She had been trying to grow some flowers just outside her door. She could dig there with no one wondering about it.

But she waited until it was dark, then dug a hole. The ground was so hard she took the gold from the bucket and put it in an old flower sack and wrapped it with string. Then it was easier to get in the ground and covered. Over the spot she put three colorful rocks she had found in the prairie. It was good enough to fool Garland Oliver.

Inside her quarters she took out the sauce pan from the back of the small cupboard and looked at the gold coins. She had kept out five of them to touch and feel and play with. A hundred dollars! That was more than half a year's pay!

She was humming when her husband, Ira, came in just before supper time. He had been on stable duty today and he hated it.

"Nothing but shoveling out horse turds and dirty straw," he always said. He was a small man, with a drooping moustache, thinning hair and a left arm with rheumatism from too many damp, cold nights in the field.

"What the hell are you so happy for? You fuck a general or something this afternoon?" he bellowed at her.

"I get happy over other things, too, Ira. But no, I didn't lift my skirts this afternoon. I just worked my cunny off."

"And that makes you happy?"

"I'm still thinking about going in to Austin for a week or so."

"Not enough army pricks out here for you, Ellie?" He spat on the wooden floor. "Christ, once a damn whore, always a floozie. I should have known better."

"You loved me, remember."

"Yeah, five years ago when I had peach

fuzz on my cheeks. I didn't know any better. You took me for a sucker. I'm not eighteen anymore."

"I am! I'm getting younger and prettier every day."

"Bullshit! You're getting sloppy and fat and in another two years you'll be paying the privates if they'll squeeze your tits."

Ellie flounced away to the back of the one big room. Maybe she would go to Austin anyway. She could sew twenty of the gold coins in the lining of an old coat she had, or maybe forty. A dozen trips and she'd have all the gold in the Austin bank! She was sure that Major Zachery would search everyone leaving the post until the gold was found. But he wouldn't know about linings.

She smiled as she started making their evening meal.

Two days later, Lieutenant Oliver returned with the patrol. They had seen and chased a wandering band of Indians, but could not identify them. The six braves may have been an advance party of some sort, or simply hunters. Oliver reported that one of the hostiles was wounded but the others escaped.

In his quarters he fell on the bed for an hour before he moved. Then he washed up and at once noticed that the washstand was not in the precise location where he had left it. He pushed it aside and checked the hiding place.

"Gone! Be damned, she did it!"

He sat there on the floor, alternately pounding the planks with his fists, and thinking of all the deadly tortures he was going to use on Ellie Unru. When he had calmed down enough to be rational, he stepped outside, grabbed the first trooper he could find and ordered him to go find Ellie Unru, the cleaning woman, and tell her to come to his quarters at once to clean his room.

Oliver stood beside his window to the parade grounds watching the enlisted men's quarters across the way. At last he saw Ellie as she came from her door and walked the long way around under the small porches built out in front of some of the areas, until she got to his door.

She knocked and waited. He let her in and saw she had her bucket and broom.

As soon as she closed the door and set down the bucket he grabbed her around the throat and squeezed hard.

She choked and gagged and tried to talk.

"You bitch! You thieving cunt! You stole my gold! I'm going to have the pleasure of ripping you apart before I kill you. I'll do it the way the Comanches do with prisoners."

She was shaking her head at him. At last he eased up enough to let her talk.

"Didn't steal anything!" she wheezed.

He let go and hit her cheek with his open palm. She staggered across the room. He followed and hit her again, a hard slap on the side of her head that turned her half around.

"Bitch! Bitch! Bitch!"

She recovered enough to be able to talk. Her voice was still wheezing and whiskey rough.

"Didn't steal anything. You hit me again, I'll go right to Major Zachery and tell him you stole the gold and show him where you hid it. He'll believe me. He can find gold shavings and dust in that hiding spot. Now, don't touch me!"

Oliver stopped. He hadn't expected her to react this way. Maybe plead for her life, maybe strip and try to seduce him. He shook his head.

"You won't go to the major, because I'll accuse you of stealing it from me. He'll tear your quarters apart."

"Won't work, Garland. He won't find a thing, cause I didn't take your old gold. Somebody else must have found it."

"Where did you hide it, Ellie? Tell me or I'll kill you yet. Then you won't tell the major anything."

She watched him closely. He meant it. She had to change her tactics just a little. "Maybe we can work together. You help me get both of us out of here, and I'll bring the gold. Agreed?"

He stared at her, then at last nodded.

"First, there's a small item we must dispose of. My husband, Ira."

Oliver never flinched. He'd expected something like this. She needed him to get away.

"Leave him here when we ride out."

"He'd suspect something and find us. You have to kill him, quickly, tonight."

Oliver began to sweat. Shooting somebody on a patrol was easy enough, but to do in a trooper right in the fort, was a lot harder.

"No, we leave him here. Where's the gold?"

"You find out after Ira is dead. Do it tonight, or forget all about the gold and remember, I'll go straight to the major. I'm just a private's wife, a cleaning woman and ex-whore. You can't hurt me at all, Garland sweetheart. Do it tonight. He'll be drinking at the sutler's until late. Catch him coming home."

Ellie turned and walked around him to the door.

Oliver made no try to stop her.

"Remember, tonight. You kill Ira, then we can get away from here." She paused and laughed. "I might even teach you the right way to make love. God knows you need some basic training in how to please a woman." She whirled and went out the door, carrying her broom and bucket. She never looked back.

Oliver watched her go, then sat down on his bed. How had he let her get the upper hand? Yeah, he showed her where he hid the gold. Dumb! He'd sure as hell never do that again. Now he had to do as she said or he'd never see that eight thousand dollars again, and all of his big dreams were dead and buried.

He went to supper mess as usual. Only three lieutenants ate in the officer room. He didn't remember what he ate or said to the other men.

Back in his quarters he sharpened his knife, a four inch, heavy bladed hunting knife he carried on his belt on patrols. That evening he was in and out of the sutler's combination store and saloon twice. He saw trooper Unru there the second time. He was playing cards for matches and buttons and drinking steadily.

Good. A drunk would be easier to approach and to fool. There was no moon. The middle of the deserted parade grounds might be the best spot to slit his throat. No, he had to make it look like an Indian raid.

Back in his quarters he found the two Indian arrows he had picked up at the Buffalo Creek wagon train massacre, and a tomahawk with a steel blade fitted tightly into the wrappings. He would use the tomahawk, leave it in Unru's skull. That way it would pinpoint the blame and keep any suspicion off him.

It should work.

He made one more trip to the sutler, bought a new deck of cards, made sure Unru was still there and went back to his quarters. He carried the arrows and tomahawk under his shirt, as he slouched in the darkness near the sutler's waiting for Unru.

It was nearly midnight by the Big Dipper clock in the sky, when Unru reeled out the door with a buddy. They sang a bawdy song as they staggered across the parade ground.

Unru stopped and urinated, and they both laughed. The other man headed for the bachelor enlisted quarters and Unru turned toward his end of the barracks.

Oliver caught Unru half way across the one hundred yard wide parade ground. He called softly and the trooper spun around.

"Unru, is that you?" Oliver asked.

Unru squinted at him. Then saw the bars

on his shoulders and started to salute.

"Yeah, yes sir. Private Unru, sir."

"No saluting, soldier. I've got a small job I want you to help me with. Come along."

The alcohol could not dull Unru's training to follow orders immediately, and without question. He turned and walked back toward the middle of the parade grounds beside the officer.

No one else was about. The interior guards were patrolling the inside of the fort's long rows of buildings. Most of them were not extremely alert either.

The center of the parade grounds was deathly dark.

Oliver pulled out the tomahawk and pointed toward the stables.

"See over there near the stable area, Unru. We've had a report of some Indian activity."

The enlisted man looked where he was told. It was the last act of his life. Oliver slammed the Indian hatchet down with much more force than was necessary. The sharp steel blade drove into Private Unru's skull, penetrated to the handle and pounded the trooper to the ground.

He had died instantly.

Oliver dropped one of the arrows, broke the second in half and left it a short distance away, then walked quickly toward the least busy section of the fort, the area that would be finished soon for guests and the stables. He met no one. That was good.

He shuddered slightly. It had been little harder than shooting that meddling sergeant. He grinned. It had been easy! Now what had been a mountainous problem had been solved. He got to his quarters quickly, went inside and bolted the door, then washed and slipped into his bed.

He wondered how quickly the body would be found. There was no guard post that covered the middle of the parade ground so the body might not be found before sunup.

Oliver lay awake for two hours trying to decide if he should go to Denver or San Francisco to start his new life. There would be more opportunity in either town. New money was not a hindrance there as it would be in New York or Boston. Yes, he would go west, and he was leaning toward San Francisco. He had never been there.

He could ride part way on the new railroad, even though it hadn't made it all the way to the West Coast yet. He had never ridden far on a train. It would be interesting.

Strange about the Indian raid that must have just taken place. None of the sentries saw a thing. Why would the Indian penetrate to the middle of the parade ground and kill one drunk trooper on his way home from a night of drinking? Strange questions, but the Comanches were strange people.

No, they were not people, they were savages. They would never be people, they were hostiles, with no regard for human life, no civilization, no morals, no manners. They were truly savages. The quicker the army could wipe them off the face of the continent, the better.

Chapter 14

Laughing Golden Hair snuggled deep into the soft warm fur of the buffalo calf. The skin had been taken in December, when the short hair had grown heavy and lush to form the absolutely prime coat. It was the softest, warmest of all the robes the small white girl gathered around her.

She had been with the Comanche now for almost a month. She was beginning to feel at home with them. True, she did miss her other mother, but her Indian mother, Cries In The Morning, had been so kind and gentle, had taught her many words of the People and shown her how to do dozens of things around the tipi.

Laughing Golden Hair was glad the band was not moving again. She had been frightened when the blue shirts had charged into the camp. She remembered little of it except the booming of the guns and the screams of the People.

She didn't understand why she lived in a different lodge now. Running Wolf, her mother's husband had gone away somewhere. Her mother tried to explain it to her, but Cries In The Morning had started crying and Laughing Golden Hair couldn't understand the words.

Now they lived in a bigger lodge, where there were two other women and two girls she could play with, and a warrior. His name was White Eagle, she had learned that. He was the leader of the Eagle band of Comanches, but everyone called them the People.

For a moment before the others in the lodge woke up, she became Sadie Harding again. She thought of her soft, blue-eyed mother with the long golden hair like her own, the gentle way she had held Sadie and sang to her. The exciting times she told them they would have when they got to the fort where her daddy worked.

It seemed like only yesterday, and then again it seemed like a very long time ago. She blinked back tears remembering the gun shots and the screams of the horses and the hollering by the troops and the Indians.

She wondered if Yale was all right. Often they had played "dead" falling down where they were. But after the game was over they got up and went on playing. She never did see Yale get up after he ran at the big Indian who threw their mother out of the covered wagon.

She did not connect the big Indian with White Eagle. That bad man had hurt Yale and her mother. He had hurt her arms too, and tied her over his back. But most of all, he had his face painted all black and he looked ugly.

Cries In The Morning rolled over on the soft buffalo robes that lay around the outer edge of the big tipi. They were on the sides of the covering that came to the ground and inward, so the cold and wetness would stay outside.

Cries In The Morning smiled when she saw her new daughter was awake.

"Hi, tai, you-oh-hobt pa-pi. Toquet?"

Laughing Golden Hair smiled and bobbed her head. She had understood all the words. Her new mother said, Hello friend yellow hair, is everything all right?

"Toquet," Laughing Golden Hair said. She had not yet learned the words for going potty.

She stood and put on her small breechclout and pointed to the tent flap.

Cries In The Morning understood, rose and took her small charge out to relieve herself. It was so good to have these small mothering duties again. It had been so long.

White Eagle saw them leave. He smiled. He had not known the small yellow hair would be in his lodge when he brought her back. It was well. She would be a chief's woman someday, perhaps his own son's woman. If he had a son.

Talks A Lot was due anytime. The women were ready, the birth lodge had been prepared.

He watched his two wives sleeping. They had found a new camp that was safe. The council had made sure of it. They had talked about it for two days, and at last they had decided and the pipe had been smoked and all had agreed to abide by the decision.

From now on, all of the warriors would be used as lookouts and sentinels to keep the camp safe. It was part of their regular duty. They would man lookouts for three day's journey in the two most dangerous directions, and one day's journey in the other two.

Never again would the people be surprised in their robes, sleeping while the enemy white-eyes charged into the camp with guns blazing.

White Eagle went out to the horse pasture and whistled for Flying Wind. For two hours he worked with the young war pony, drumming into his quick mind every motion, every movement that White Eagle wanted, using only his knees, his legs and feet to guide the pony. When he was satisfied with the colt's progress, he took him to a patch of thistles the young horse loved and let him eat.

Back at the lodge, Cries In The Morning had spread out the last buffalo skin her late husband had shot on the hunt. She had scraped it once, but now it needed a second scraping to remove more of the fat and bits of flesh from the skinning. It had to be smooth and nearly the same thickness all over.

She used a metal scraper made from the blade of a hoe that Running Wolf had stolen on one of the raids.

Laughing Golden Hair had tired of playing with White Eagle's two daughters in the lodge, and sat near the big hide as her mother scraped. Soon she found another scraper, a smaller one and worked on the side of the skin.

Always Smiling came and watched for a moment, then shook her head and took the scraper and showed Laughing Golden Hair how to do it properly. The small white girl pouted for a minute, but when she saw how the older woman did it and how gently, she took back the tool and smiled.

Sadie realized she had never been scolded once since she came to the People. She had not been spanked or disciplined in any way. She couldn't remember any of the children being spanked or scolded.

When the little boys got too rambunctious their parents simply told them that was not the way the People acted. It was the sharpest reprimand they received. They seemed to grow up free and happy, but with respect and love for their parents.

Little Sadie wondered again about her mother. She frowned trying to remember exactly how she looked. The long golden hair was easy, but it was becoming harder to remember her mother's soft, pretty face.

Her father was easier, because they had pictures of him to look at. And Yale was easy. She wondered how bad Yale had been hurt when he played dead!

Her two new sisters came and caught her hand. They were going to find berries. She looked at Cries In The Morning who smiled and nodded.

The three girls ran off, each wearing the small breechclouts. Laughing Golden Hair had her hair greased and braided so it wouldn't get in her way. Her skin had taken on a pleasant tan, so she was much darker than when she arrived, but still a shade or two lighter than her sisters.

They ran to the stream, waded in it for a minute, then hurried to some tall bushes that had black colored berries. The others girls ate a few, so Laughing Golden Hair tried one. It was good! Almost like the wild blackberries she used to eat. They had brought small baskets, and picked enough berries to fill two of them, then took them back to the lodge and hurried again to the stream.

"Swimming," the oldest girl who was just past six, said to Laughing Golden Hair in Comanche, but she didn't understand. She caught the smaller girl's hand and they stepped into the water.

Then the two Indian girls took off their breechclouts and dropped naked into the cool water. Sadie felt white again as she watched them. Her mother had told her . . . What had it been about not taking off her clothes? She shrugged. Her sisters did it. She loosened her breechclout and dropped it on the shore and ran into the water, screeching at the chill, then falling into the coolness and laughing with the others.

They played until they were chilled, splashing and dunking their heads under, then rushing out to a grassy place and lying in the sun to dry themselves and get warm again.

As she lay there half dozing, she thought about the Pony Soldiers whom she had seen galloping into the village. Her real father was a soldier! What if he had been with the other Pony Soldiers looking for her? She had not cried out to tell him where she was.

She frowned. She wondered if her daddy would come and get her? But Cries In The Morning had run off with her, hid her away from the Pony Soldiers. As Sadie, she was confused. Didn't Cries In The Morning know she wanted to find her daddy again? She would try to tell her. She would learn more of the words so they could talk together better. With the girls she didn't need to know as many words.

She sat up and suddenly realized she was naked. She put on her breechclout and felt better.

Soon the three girls were playing tag. When they tired of that they hit a round leather ball stuffed with buffalo hair. They used sticks and tried to hit it past the other team. When they had enough of that, they went back and picked more of the black berries and ate them.

Wash her hair! Sadie remembered that her

mother used to wash her hair every Saturday night. She hadn't thought about the days of the week for a long, long time. She wondered what day it was? It didn't matter here.

She wanted to wash her hair.

Laughing Golden Hair began to unbraid her hair. She left the other girls and ran for the stream, taking off her breechclout again she hurried into the water, sat down and ducked her head again with her hair loose and flying. She washed it carefully, using sand from the bottom to wash the buffalo grease from her hair. She washed it three times as the other girls watched.

When she rinsed all of the sand away she felt cleaner than she had been in days and days. She sat on the shore, put on her breechclout and let her hair dry in the sun. She looked in a quiet pool and saw her blonde hair dry into a fluffy halo around her head.

It felt so good that way for a change.

Back at the tipi, Cries In The Morning looked at her new daughter and laughed, then combed out the long blonde hair, greased it and braided it again, talking all the time, laughing and letting Laughing Golden Hair know she had not done a bad thing. It was simply better braided this way.

That was when Sadie let the tears roll down her cheeks as she cried softly. She wanted to go home. She wanted to see her mother and father, and even Yale.

She wanted to go home!

The tears came freely then and Cries In The Morning looked surprised, then hugged her gently and crooned a soft lullaby.

Chapter 15

At 7:15 A.M. Major Zachery stormed into Captain Harding's office. His shirt was buttoned crooked, his hair still rumpled and there was a snarl on his face.

"Harding, what the hell is going on this morning? What's this about an Indian attack?"

Captain Harding leaned back in his chair, slowly locked his fingers together behind his neck and stared at the only man on the post who outranked him.

"And a good morning to you, too, Major. I've been up since a little after three A.M. when the body was found. I've been trying to figure it out myself ever since.

"About three this morning a guard cut across the parade ground and stumbled over the body of Private Ira Unru. Killed with a tomahawk. Two Indian arrows were found in the vicinity. We can find no other loss, damage or sign of any Indian intrusion. How would you call it?"

"Just one body? Doesn't sound like Comanches. Any horses stolen?"

"Not a one, not a bridal, not a round of ammunition. I don't think it was an Indian attack either. But someone wants us to think it was."

"Maybe it's tied in with the stolen gold?"

"Maybe. More likely Unru said the wrong thing to the wrong trooper last night at his regular drinking bout, and that person more than evened the score. We're searching out just who was in the sutler's saloon last night, and if there were any fights."

"Sounds like work. I'm going to have my breakfast."

"I had mine. Take your time. This probably has nothing to do with your missing gold."

"Unru did you say? The name sounds familiar."

"Been here almost a year, first hitch, but an average trooper these days."

Major Zachery waved and left for the officer's mess. As he did, the sutler came in. His name was Hans Altzanger, a German immigrant who ran a fine store on the post and a small saloon area for the drinkers. Hans held his cloth cap in his hands, twisting it nervously.

"You wanted see me, sir?"

"Hans, yes, come in and sit down. You heard about the problem?"

"Unru, yes, good customer. But he drink too much. I tell him. Last night I not sell him more."

"You cut him off? Did that make him angry?"

"No, he had others buy for him."

"Did he get in any brawls, any fights last night?"

"No fights. I not allow."

"Did Unru argue with anybody, yell and scream?"

"No. Others, not Unru. He a quiet drinker. Even cry sometimes. Not fighter when drunk."

Captain Harding scowled. He had been afraid of that. No good suspects. "Hans, do you remember who was in your store last night? Could you give me the names?"

"Some. Not know all names. Maybe Corporal could help. Hans describe, Corporal know name?"

"Yes, Hans. Good idea. You talk to Corporal Swenson, I want the names as soon as you can remember them."

The store man went to the outer office. Captain Harding marched to his small window and looked at the parade grounds. Why would a private, a married private, be murdered?

He knew the stories about Mrs. Unru, Ellie. She was what some commanders called an "available" woman on post. Some isolated forts and posts with no wives on board, even brought in two or three fancy ladies for the entertainment of the troops.

Often the wives of enlisted men did laundry and housecleaning for the men and for officers. Quite naturally some of the women were not offended by making a few dollars extra to help with the family budget.

Mrs. Unru had been mainly an "officers" woman. Two of the enlisted men's wives had a clientele among the enlisted swains.

He rubbed his chin. Unru didn't seem to mind that his wife whored around. Why would somebody get mad at him for his wife's loose living? Not reasonable. Maybe the other way? Unru objected to someone laying his wife and . . . no not likely. He was right back where he began.

Corporal Swenson came in the door.

"Captain, sir. We have a list of ten names. The others will be harder. Thought you might want to start to talk to some of the ones we have."

Harding nodded and took the sheet of paper. He looked down the list and stopped at the bottom one, Lieutenant Oliver's name was on the list. He went to the outer office and up to Altzanger.

"Hans, Lieutenant Oliver was drinking last night?"

"Oh, no sir. He bought new deck cards. Said had heard about new solitaire. His desk missing card."

"I see. So he didn't stay very long?"

"Just few minutes. He look around, leave."

"Thanks, Hans. You keep working on that list."

Five minutes later Major Zachery opened Colt Harding's office door and stepped inside.

"Got something to show you, Captain. You might remember I said I had some suspicions about two men. I've been keeping watch on the two. So far I have a record of twelve days in a row when Lieutenant Oliver was visited by a young lady in the afternoon, in the evening, once after taps."

"Some men are younger than we are, Major. Been a good long time that I've had a woman every day for twelve days."

"True, but the name of this woman is what makes it interesting. Her name is Ellie Unru."

Captain Harding turned quickly. "Damn interesting. Here's a list of some of the men who were in the sutler's saloon last night. Look at the bottom name."

"Oliver!" the major roared. "Let's arrest the bastard."

"On what charges, buying a deck of cards or fucking the post officers' whore?"

"He wanted to get rid of Unru so he could take over the woman."

"Major, you've seen Ellie Unru. She isn't the kind to drive men to murder. And Oliver isn't the kind to go overboard for a cheap whore like Ellie Unru. We need some proof."

"It still could tie in with the missing gold."

"Legally 'could' is the weakest word in the book. We still need evidence."

"I want your permission to search the quarters of Lieutenant Oliver and Mrs. Unru. That's where we'll find enough proof to scare them into confessing."

"Some commanders might operate that way, Major, but I never have, especially with my officers. Out here we put our lives on the line for each other a dozen times a year. I don't want any mistrust between my officers. We do it another way."

"What other way?"

"I don't know. We trap them somehow, trick them. We need some kind of a plan."

"When you get one, let me know," the major said sarcastically. "I'm fresh out of clever plans."

"Oliver is still just a suspect. I'm waiting for the full list of men in the saloon last night. We might find a much better suspect."

"Try this story," Major Zachery said. "Oliver steals the gold, hides it in his quarters. His regular cleaning lady finds it and confronts him. He says he'll marry her and run away. She beds him for two weeks, then changes her mind, steals the gold from Oliver and hides it. Now, she says kill my husband and run away with me with the gold, or I'll go to the captain and tell him you stole the gold. Over a barrel, Oliver does in her husband. Which brings us up to now."

"Work good in a dime novel, Major, but I'm still looking for the facts. Even if we arrested Oliver, we don't have a shred of evidence to use in a court martial."

"He'll confess, and we won't need evidence."

"Oliver would confess only to save his neck from a noose."

"So what the hell can we do now?"

"I'll conduct an investigation, talk to the men at the saloon, not let on to Oliver he's even a suspect, and maybe we'll get lucky. He might head out of the fort some dark night. If he does, I'll have a man watching his door and we'll know. Then we'll grab him. Otherwise, we watch and wait."

By noon Captain Harding was hard at questioning the men individually who had been at the sutler's last night. He got no help in his quest. There had been no fights, almost no arguments, and the two people who really argued were not involved with Unru at all. He sat in a corner nursing one beer after another, until he left with a friend who had no reason at all to kill the slight private.

By supper call, Captain Harding had discovered no new facts, and nothing to help him. He called in Major Zachery.

"I have a suggestion. I'm asking Ellie Unru to come to my office in about fifteen minutes. I'll keep her here for half an hour. That will give you plenty of time to search her quarters. I won't know anything about it. Deal?"

The major grinned and left the room at once.

Ellie Unru was nervous as she sat in the outer office waiting for the captain to talk to her. He kept her waiting for twenty minutes, then asked her in.

"Mrs. Unru, first let me tell you how sorry we all are here at Camp Comfort about your loss. It's a tragic murder. No Indians were involved, and we're trying the best we can to discover who killed your husband."

She wept silently into a handkerchief clutched in her left hand.

"Mrs. Unru, would you have any idea who might have hated your husband, who might have wanted to do him harm? Did he owe anyone a gambling debt, for instance?"

"No sir. Mr. Ira never gambled. He drank some, but he said he needed it for his rheumatiz. He was a kind man. Not really educated or smart, but kind."

They talked for another five minutes, then Captain Harding gave her the list of men from the saloon to check over. She looked at each one and shook her head.

"None of these men would want to harm my Ira. I just don't know who it was."

"What are your plans now, Mrs. Unru? You won't be able to stay in the married enlisted quarters."

"I . . . I thought of that. I guess I'll go into Austin. I have a friend living there. I really haven't planned much."

"No hurry. But within a month we need to know what you'll be doing."

They talked a few more minutes, then Captain Harding stood and escorted her out of his office.

Ten minutes later Major Zachery came in, a smile on his face. He closed the office door, and held his closed hand out to Harding.

"Never guess what I found in the poor widow's quarters." He opened his hand.

A bright, shining double eagle lay there. Harding looked at the mint date. It was 1869, a coin that had not been issued yet and was not due out until the following month. It must have come from the box of stolen coins.

Captain Harding smiled. 'So we have a good suspect. That's still not enough evidence to arrest her. Where did you find it?"

"It was under a small couch, as if it had fallen and rolled under there and she didn't miss it. Not to miss two months pay for an enlisted man's wife is not normal. She must have had three hundred and ninety eight other coins like it to play with."

"Maybe," Harding said. "How did she get them? That's what we have to prove. Also we'll need those other coins. If she's hidden them, we could play old billy hell in convincing her to show us where they are."

"That will be the job of the court martial," Major Zachery insisted. "I still say Oliver stole it, she used her body to sex him up and get a look at the gold, then she stole it. Now she's got him doing her dirty work for her . . . like murder. That makes her guilty of murder, too. I say we arrest them right now, before either one can make a run for it."

Chapter 16

When Ellie Unru stepped out of the captain's office, she felt a slight shiver go down her back bone. The Fort Commander knew more than he was letting on. Somehow she was suspect in Ira's murder and probably the stolen gold as well.

She walked stiffly and slowly, befitting a new widow. Ira's burial would be the next afternoon. There was no way to put it off another day with the warm weather. Just as well.

When she came toward her quarters, she looked at the three colored rocks she had placed over the spot where she buried the gold. All were in precisely the place she had put them. If they had been moved, nobody could have put them back the same way.

She walked past the spot and went in her door. She never locked it. There was nothing to steal inside. Most of the enlisted men left their doors unlocked.

At once she sensed movement behind her and whirled to find Garland Oliver standing behind the door as she closed it.

His face was red with anger. She had never

seen him so worked up, not even when they made love. For a moment more he couldn't speak, then he flew at her and she jumped aside to get out of his way.

"What did you tell the captain?"

She watched him for a moment. His panic/fear attack had passed. He was gaining control of himself.

"Calm down, Garland. I told him what he wanted to hear, that I had no idea who could have killed a wonderful man like Ira. That he had no enemies, owed no one money, didn't gamble and was as pure as the driven snow. You shouldn't be here."

"Why?"

"Because everyone knows I've been sleeping with you. Now my husband is murdered. Not too hard to make a connection, even though it ain't true."

He frowned and bobbed his head. "Damned if you aren't right. But I have some news for you. The minute you stepped inside the captain's office, Major Zachery came into your quarters. He was here for twenty minutes. Has anything been moved? Did he search the place?"

She gasped and looked around. The furniture, what there was of it, was in about the same position. She looked in her dresser drawer. Yes, it had been searched. Things were the same, but a little different. As if a hand had crept through them looking for gold coins.

"Did he find any gold coins?" Oliver asked her, his voice shrill, tight.

"No, it isn't in here. I just had a couple and I . . . I sewed them in the lining of my coat." She looked in the closet and came out with it, showing the round lumps where the coins nestled in thick seams along the buttons.

"He must have found one coin. That darnned major looked pleased as a pussycat eating cream when he left your door. He went directly to the captain's office."

"Oh, Lord! I did drop some one night, but I picked them all up. I think."

"You think! God, woman, I could be facing a hanging here, you too! Don't you realize . . . ?" He stopped, took a long, deep breath and looked out the front wide window into the parade ground.

"All right. It's time. We'll leave tonight as soon as it gets dark. You get the gold wherever you hid it, and I'll walk by and we'll stroll to the gate. I'll have two horses there and we'll bribe the sentry, telling him we're going to the stream to make love in the water. He'll believe it."

"And we won't come back," she added

smiling.

"True, we won't. All you have to do is get the gold and put on about two sets of clothes so you'll be warm enough to ride through the night for Austin."

She hesitated. Was there any other way? She searched her mind. If the major had found that one gold coin she lost, the whole thing would come crashing down quickly.

"Oh, put the gold in some kind of a picnic basket, and put food on the top. We'll tell the sentry it's a late supper as well."

"Yes, it should work. I can't think of any other way."

"Believe me, Ellie, I've been trying to come up with a better plan ever since I saw Major Zachery slip into your quarters here. Believe me, this is best. Now, you go out and water your flowers or something, so I can ease out and get away without making a big announcement of my visit."

She did, leaving the door open. She was careful not to get the rocks wet covering the gold sack. When she turned around she saw Oliver walking casually down the side of the quadrangle toward the officers' quarters. She turned and went back inside for more water, then shook her head at the daisies. She didn't think they were going to bloom after all.

Oliver figured he was being watched.

There was no way that Major Zachery had not pegged him as the prime suspect in the gold robbery. And now the "coincidence" of the woman he was bedding getting her husband killed, would make the suspicion that much tighter.

He stopped in at Lieutenant Edwards' quarters and found the officer alone. His wife was playing cards in another part of the fort.

"Dan, need a small favor," Oliver said when he was invited in. He and Dan had got along fine recently.

"Yeah, figures. Anybody but my wife."

They both laughed.

"Along those lines. I got a wild one set for tonight. I told you I poke Ellie now and then. Tonight I want to surprise her and take her down by the stream and get her bare ass in the grass in the moonlight."

"You'll have to talk to Ellie about that, I'd say."

"Not the problem. I need somebody to set up two horses and saddles out by the front fence of the paddock. Just down from the front gate. Won't be any trouble with the gate sentry. I'll tell him we're off on a moonlight walk and slip him a silver dollar."

Dan Edwards laughed. "Garland, why don't you just get married and you can have it every night? No more wild schemes."

"The schemes are what keep it fun. Can you do it?"

"Hell yes. Do I want to?"

"So I'll owe you a favor. Come on. I got big plans for her tonight."

"Okay, why not. Just don't get me in trouble."

"Not a chance. Now, I've got to put my first platoon through its paces."

He did. For the next three hours, Oliver drilled his first platoon relentlessly. Major Zachery watched them in the parade ground, then saw them go on a half mile ride outside the fort and return. This line officer knew men, could get them to do what he needed them to do. Too bad he was also a thief, and probably a cold blooded murderer as well.

Oliver had supper in the mess and went back to his quarters. There he stripped to his waist and in the washbowl took a sponge bath from the waist up. Then he put on a clean uniform, and slid his service revolver in his shirt. Yes, it would work in the dark.

Now, if that damned woman would dig up the gold he would be ready. She had bought the story. She wanted to believe him. Once they were two miles down the trail to Austin, the poor lady would suffer a serious and fatal accident.

The secret was for her to believe him

enough to bring out the gold from wherever she had hidden it. He'd make damn sure by looking in the bag before they left. They would meet at the gate. By the time they were out, and the private who had been watching him reported back to Major Zachery, they would have enough of a head start. Not even Colt Harding could track him in the dark!

He had drilled his troops that afternoon to throw the good major off the scent. It also gave him something to do to stay busy. Now it was a half hour to dark. He stepped outside and looked across the corner of the buildings where he could see Ellie's door. He went back inside and concentrated on the small window, but he didn't see her come out of her door.

When it was full dark, he turned up his shirt collar, pulled his hat down over his face and walked past her door. He could hear her humming inside. He wanted to knock, but knew he shouldn't.

Twenty minutes later from the darkness of the parade ground, he saw her door open. There was no lamp burning inside. He saw her shadowy figure bend over the flower bed and start to dig.

Yes! he should have guessed it. He gave her time to get the gold, then walked up quickly as she stepped inside her darkened door.

She yelped as he pushed her inside and went with her. Then saw it was him. Inside she showed him the picnic basket. She lit a lamp and kept it low. He unrolled the sack and found the gold coins and saw them glint in the low lamplight.

There was no reason to leave with her. He had the gold. He had what he wanted.

He slipped his .44 from his shirt and held it by the barrel. When she turned he slammed the butt of the heavy gun down hard on Ellie's skull. He heard it crack. She sighed and fell.

He saw the blood gushing from her skull, staining her hair, then her blouse. He had to finish it. He gritted his teeth and hit her twice more, then again. Each time the bloody handle of his pistol sank deeper into her skull. It fascinated him. He took one last look at all that was left of Ellie before he blew out the lamp.

Oliver put the sack of gold coins inside his shirt, knowing that they made an obscene bulge.

But it was the best he could do. He pushed the .44 on top of the sack, moved a box of shells in his front pocket and slipped out the door.

It was a short way down to the entrance to the paddock through the fort wall. When the square was finished, it would be only one of two openings.

At the paddock gate he talked with the private on guard duty.

"Need to check on my mount. She seemed to have a bad foot this afternoon. I'll look her over and if it's bad, I'll bring her back up here where you have a lantern."

"Yes, sir Lieutenant Oliver. Your mount should be down near the gate end of the paddock."

Oliver thanked the private and walked into the dark corral that was fenced on three sides and walled in by the fort on the fourth. He walked along the building to the fence near the front of the fort and saw the two horses waiting for him outside the barrier. Quickly he stepped through the wire, and led the two saddled mounts slowly and quietly away from the fort toward Austin. No one could see him in the darkness.

With any luck he would be half way to Austin before they knew he was gone. He walked out five hundred yards, then tied the reins of the second horse onto his saddle in a lead line, mounted the first horse and rode away at a walk down the dark trail toward Austin. He knew the route by heart. A hundred and twenty miles.

He remembered he had no food or

supplies. But he had his pistol. Perhaps he could shoot a rabbit.

A half mile away from the fort, he lifted the mount to a canter and moved out swiftly. He would ride one horse until it was tired out, then transfer to the other one. That way he could easily outdistance any mounted pursuit that had only one horse each.

Oliver grinned in the soft moonlight. *Mister Oliver*, that was! He was a rich civilian who would discard his army duds just as quick as he could!

Back at Fort Comfort, Private Freddy Daniels followed Oliver as far as the enlisted barracks. He had no idea why the officer had stood in the dark parade ground for so long. Then he slipped into one of the enlisted men's dependent quarters and was there for a short time.

He came out and went to the paddock, and talked with the stable sentry. That was when Daniels went to see Major Zachery.

"You said he went to the dependents' quarters and stayed a time, then went to the paddock?"

"Yes sir. He talked with the sentry. Something about checking his mount."

"I don't like that, Daniels. Was it Ellie Unru's quarters he visited?"

"Yes sir. Maybe three or four minutes."

"Then the light came on, went out and he left?"

"Yes sir."

"I'll check the paddocks, Daniels. I want you to go to the front gate and remind the sentries there they are not to allow Oliver to leave the area."

"Yes sir."

Major Zachery put on his gunbelt and checked his issue .44 pistol, then walked across the parade grounds from his quarters to the paddock. Instead of going straight there, he went to the dependents' quarters and located the Unru door. The room was dark. He knocked.

There was no response. He knocked again. The door had not been locked or latched and it edged open. Major Zachery pushed it inward. A strange odor touched his senses.

He found matches in his pocket and struck one on the door and held it high.

On the floor almost at his feet lay Ellie Unru. Blood oozed and matted in her hair. The whole top and side of her skull had been smashed in. There was no chance she could be alive.

He rushed outside.

"Corporal of the Guard!" he bellowed. "Corporal of the Guard. Dependents' quarters, on the double!"

He raced along the doorways to the opening where the paddock was. The sentry there was alert and saluted smartly.

"Challenge me, damnit, don't salute!" the major shouted. "Did Lieutenant Oliver come in here a few minutes ago?"

"Yes sir. He's in the paddock, checking his horse."

"That's what he said he was going to do. Get me a lantern, quickly!"

The private started to leave.

"Idiot, you can't leave your post. Stay here."

"Corporal of the Guard, the paddock!" Major Zachery bellowed. He heard it repeated down the line. Somebody bolted from the guard room with a pair of lanterns.

"When they get here, send them into the paddock." Major Zachery ran in among the free horses. They moved grudgingly where they slept standing up. He ran to the fence and patrolled around it. He fully expected to find it cut where Oliver had taken a horse and ridden off.

The fence was not cut. He grabbed a lantern from the Corporal of the Guard and ordered him to go tell Captain Harding his presence was requested by the major.

By the time Captain Harding got his boots and pants on, and went out to the paddock,

Major Zachery had it figured out.

He pointed to the horse droppings outside the fence.

"Two mounts! They must have been here for at least two hours. Oliver got the gold, killed Ellie Unru, came through the paddock, went through the fence and rode away with his gold and an extra horse."

"For once, I think you're right, Major Zachery," Harding said. He turned and spoke to his orderly.

"Swenson, dig out Sergeant Casemore. Tell him to get dressed for a ride."

Back at the sentry post at the paddock gate, he ordered another trooper to get four of the best horses out of the paddock and saddle all four.

"I want rations for four days and blanket rolls for two riders. Make it as fast as you can, soldier."

"We going after him?" Major Zachery asked.

"No, Major, Sgt. Casemore and I are going after him. We'll take two horses the same way he has. Now we damn well have the evidence we need."

Harding ran back to his quarters, dug out his best pair of pistols, took his Spencer repeating rifle and two hundred rounds of ammunition and went to the front porch. The four saddled horses were ready.

Casemore came running up. He had borrowed a Spencer and shoved it in the saddle boot.

"Ready when you are, sir," Casemore said.

They stepped on board the army mounts and galloped for the main gate, their relief horses on short lead lines behind them.

Chapter 17

Captain Harding and Sergeant Casemore rode through the front gate at a gallop and turned toward Austin.

"Only way he could have gone," Harding shouted. "He didn't have any provisions, or damn few. He could make Austin in two days of hard riding. A man can live for two days without food."

They continued the gallop for a quarter of a mile, then walked the horses for a quarter of a mile and galloped again. Three miles from the fort, in a section of the trail that went through a soft dirt spot they got off and used torches of dry weeds to search for hoof prints. They found them quickly.

"First horse is loaded with a rider and four

hundred ounces of gold," Casemore said. "That's another twenty-five pounds. The trail horse is not nearly as loaded, like only a saddle. He was walking the nags through here."

"He knows somebody will be after him, but he probably hoped it wouldn't be until morning," Captain Harding said. "What we've got to do is punish our horses more than he does. Let's ride."

They galloped their horses for a half hour, then shifted to the second mounts and galloped them for a mile and walked. The horses were both lathering, but they couldn't stop and rub them down.

Six miles from the fort they checked the trail again. By the spring back of some grass in the hoof prints, Harding decided they were less than two hours behind him.

"Just depends how hard he pushes," Casemore said. "I'd bet a dollar that he's counting on us being single mounted when we come after him. On that basis we never would catch him.

"By dawn we look for a little rise in the trail. By that time we should be close enough to see him or catch his dust trail."

"He's going to fight," Casemore said.

"True, and he's a good shot. The bastard is a marksman with a rifle and pistol, so when we get near him we play it easy. We take no chances, but we nail the bastard."

"He won't have a chance in a court martial."

"Oliver will know that. He'll be hard to bring back alive."

"Either way is fine with me," Casemore said. "He's already killed two people, and I've got suspicions about a third."

"Corporal Pendleton on that wood detail?"

"The same. Pendleton was a little bit of a schemer, but he was a damn good soldier. Not a chance he would poke his head up when some Indians could nail him. My guess is that Pendleton knew something about the gold, confronted Oliver about it, and the wood detail proved a convenient way to murder Pendleton and blame it on the Comanches."

"Figures," Captain Harding said, his face etching even grimmer as he lifted the pace to a gallop again.

They traded horses three more times before it got light. Once, about four A.M. they stopped and rubbed down both pair of mounts, fed them, watered both good, then rode again.

Daybreak found them coming out of some brushy lowlands into a slight rise. The land ahead was open and covered with buffalo grass.

Captain Harding hesitated, squinted, then growled.

"There he is, just moving toward the top of that rise. See the two horses riding slow?'

"Got to be him. Out of range."

"We don't shoot at him until we've got him in our sights at a hundred yards or less. I don't want him getting away."

Colt tested the wind. It blew in their faces, away from their quarry.

"Let's have some coffee and bacon or whatever we have for chow," Harding said. "We want him on that down slope so we can get closer."

Casemore made a small cooking fire with nearly smokeless dry branches, and Harding fried bacon and boiled coffee. With hardtack and some apples they made a quick breakfast.

They were riding twenty minutes after they stopped.

"Only way I can figure is that Oliver discovered the gold when he came up fast with me right after our lead scouts found the wagons. I saw him checking the wagons, but I was . . . was busy at the time. He could have taken the gold right then, or later when the detail dug the graves. He could even have got it the next morning when they came back for the wagons. Damn him!"

"Don't worry, sir. This won't get that far to reflect on your career. I'm sure all the major wants is the gold back in government hands. He can work up some explanation about the gold being lost or misplaced or covered up by the Indians. He seems like a reasonable man. He can get the credit, and nobody gets the blame."

"Fine by me, Sergeant Casemore. All we have to do is get the gold back, and convince the major."

They galloped up the hill and at the top eased ahead to look over. The Texas landscape spread out in front of them for a ten mile stretch in a long flat plain with hardly a lift or break.

"We go around him," Colt said. "We drift to the left, swing over half a mile and get around him fast and wait for him just about where the dark line of trees shows up there, maybe eight miles."

"He's a half mile ahead now," Casemore judged. "With any luck we should be able to go around him easy."

They angled to the left, put a half mile to one side under their hooves, then turned due east again. They galloped ten yards apart so they wouldn't create a double dust trail. There was little dust at all here in the grassy plain.

Twice they changed mounts, working the horses harder than any Cavalry officer would expect on a flat out charge. But both men knew the horses could take it, and it was the only way to outdistance the man ahead with two horses.

They hit the creek a little less than an hour later, and worked along behind the thin screen of wild almonds and a few wild cherry trees scattered through the willow. They came to the spot the wagons had forded the creek. The water level was coming down, but still ran a foot deep and twenty feet wide.

Casemore slid off his horse and checked the dust of the trail where it had been worn bare.

"He hasn't been past here yet," Casemore said. They tied their horses a hundred yards back on one side, then worked up silently through the brush until they could see the trail toward the fort.

"Got him!" Captain Harding said softly. "There, just beyond that rock off the main trail to the left. Looks like he's heading for the shade upstream a ways."

They both lifted up and faded through the brush on foot without making a sound.

Oliver shifted his angle and rode straight for the water now, ignoring the trail. He got into the brush before his trackers got to that point.

They stopped, gave him time to dismount and look around.

Both Cavalrymen had their Spencer repeaters.

"Careful," Harding whispered. "Not a sound." He motioned Casemore across the shallow stream, then they moved forward.

Ten minutes later, Captain Harding edged around a small wild pecan tree and saw the two army mounts. They had been staked out and hobbled. Both munched on fresh spring grass near the water.

On this side of them, Oliver lay on the grass, his head on his blanket roll, a canteen to his lips as he drank again and again.

It was an old Cavalry trick. If you didn't have enough to eat, drink plenty to keep your belly from screaming at you. Oliver was using the idea while he had the water.

Captain Harding had lost sight of Casemore. Right now, he didn't need him. He lifted the Spencer, aimed carefully, and sent a .56 caliber slug thunking into the tree trunk just over Oliver's head.

Oliver started to jolt away.

"Don't move, or you're dead meat!" Harding bellowed. "We've got six men around you. More than one party can use relief horses, or didn't you think of that?"

Before Harding could finish the sentence,

Oliver's hidden hand triggered a pistol sending three slugs in the captain's direction. One crashed into his left arm, spinning him away from the tree, and bringing a scream of pain and frustration from the captain.

Even as Colt slammed backwards, he heard another Spencer fire and a second scream stabbed through the quiet Texas prairie.

"Sonsofbitches!" Oliver screamed. "I should have killed you all!"

By the time Harding had pushed himself around so he could see where Oliver was, the man had moved.

A six-gun blasted again, one shot, then a spaced second shot and across the stream there came a howl of pain.

Harding braced himself with the Spencer and pushed upright beside the tree. He stared around the trunk, ignoring the throbbing in his left arm. So he was losing some blood, he had lots. This had to be finished now.

He watched the small brush and plants around the grassy area where Oliver had been. If he had rolled away, he would have stayed low. There. He would have gone that way. A small tree, two feet high was bent to the left and now slowly began straightening itself.

Harding worked the lever on his Spencer and sent three rounds smashing into the thicker brush behind the young tree. He had the lever coming back up when he saw a form lift up and surge toward a foot-thick tree.

Harding lifted the Spencer and fired without aiming, rather he pointed the weapon the way he would a finger when he had to indicate a direction or an individual quickly.

The .56 caliber slug bored from the rifle barrel, spun through the air and caught Oliver just under the heart, slicing through important body parts before it powered out his back an inch from his spinal column taking half a rib with it.

Oliver lay on his back when Captain Colt Harding eased up beside him and kicked the pistol out of his hand. His eyes were angry and tired at the same time. His left hand covered the small purple hole in his chest and he coughed, spitting up blood.

"Casemore!" Harding yelled.

"Yeah. You nail the bastard? I developed a severe case of a broken leg. Lucky round from Oliver's .44."

"Hold on, I'll be over." He turned back to Oliver. "You look a little worse for the wear. Is all the stolen gold in your four saddlebags?"

"Yes."

"You killed Private Unru, and then his widow?"

"Yes, she stole ..." he went into a violent coughing seizure and screamed as he vomited blood. Wearily he wiped the blood from his lips and turned his eyes toward Captain Harding. The blood now drenched his chest.

"She stole the gold, made me kill her husband before she'd tell me where she hid it."

"Then you arranged to ride out with her, after she dug up the gold?"

Oliver nodded.

"And Corporal Pendleton. You murdered him, too?"

"Yes. He saw me take the gold."

"Why all of this, Oliver? You were a good soldier, a good officer. You could have had a fine career."

"Temptation, too much of a temptation. Haven't you ever wanted to be rich?"

"Not that bad, Oliver."

Captain Harding stood and went over to the creek to Casemore. The non-com had his leg half splinted. The break was below the knee.

Colt helped tie the branches in place using his own kerchief and then his belt to tighten it solidly.

Casemore screeched in pain as they stood.

Harding lifted him on his back and carried him across the creek. He helped him sit down against a tree without hurting the leg again.

The commanding officer went back to look at Oliver. His face was ashen.

"Lost too much blood. Hole in my back big as my fist. Family going to be embarrassed. They were the end of old money. Couldn't you clean up this whole matter a little for them?"

"Comanche raid?" Captain Harding asked.

"Why not? You've got the gold. I'll be dead in five minutes. Why should my family suffer?"

Colt Harding looked at him. The man had a point.

Oliver gasped, his eyes went wide, then he screamed and blood spewed from his mouth. He lifted half way to a sitting position, then fell on his side, a long, soft gush of air escaping from his lungs that would never breathe again.

Casemore spat on the ground and shook his head.

"Captain, sir. You're not going to let the murdering bastard get away with it, are you?"

Captain Harding reached over and took the man's shoulders and eased him back to the ground. It had been a long time since he had dug a soldier's grave. He watched Lieutenant Garland Oliver's face now in repose but still looked to be suffering.

"He paid for what he did, Casemore. Paid about as much as any man can pay. Why should his parents and brothers suffer? They live in Boston. That can be a ridiculously straight laced group back there."

That was when Captain Harding realized that they didn't have a shovel. Casemore tied up the Captain's wounded arm.

"Let's think about it on the way back. We can't bury him here. If the gold is in those two saddle bags, I think I can convince the major to scratch this all out smooth and even. Hell, the Comanches have been known to raid in this close, they even hit Austin once a couple of years ago. Nobody can swear they weren't in here again."

Casemore shrugged. He'd been in the army long enough to ride with the punches.

"Captain, you get me back to the fort where Doc can set my leg, and I'll go along with any report you want to write up." Casemore grinned. "Course, you might have to play my orderly for the next couple of days – help me mount my horse, cook my meals for me, simple things like that."

Captain Harding grinned. "I'd thought of leaving you out here with Oliver, but you're so damn mean you'd probably hop all the way back to the fort alone and on one foot. I guess I can be your orderly for a couple of days."

He went to Oliver's two army mounts and checked the gold. The bags were stuffed with gold double eagles. He freed the mount and lifted into the saddle of one, then rode slowly over to where Casemore lay.

"I'll go get our horses. We might as well get half a day's ride in before it gets dark. You up to moving a few miles down the trail?"

An hour later they were riding slowly back down the trail toward Fort Comfort. Every step of the trip bounced Casemore's leg and sent rivers of pain into his brain, but he wasn't about to complain. He was alive. Behind him on the third lead horse, Oliver was spread face down over his saddle, his hands and feet tied together under the mount's belly.

Harding grimaced at the hot sun as he moved along the trail. They would drop off Oliver two hour's ride from Fort Comfort and send out a burial detail. Then he would tackle Major Zachery and the gold problem. He thought he could win it and let Oliver's people live in peace.

He looked northwest.

Up there somewhere his baby girl was a captive of the Comanche. He would not rest until he found the right combination of information and troop movement to have another chance to attack the Eagle Band of the Comanches. This time he would do it right. He would slip in on the Indians quietly, and alone. He would find his daughter and slip away before they knew he was there!

It had to work.

It was his dream, it was his reason for living. He would get his daughter back from the Comanches or he would die trying!